Pete Palamountain

RUNAWAY TWINS

With the help of a rebellious boy,
twin girls flee a polygamous cult in mid-winter
Montana

CONTENTS

Chapter

1 ....A Run for Freedom

2 ....Act of Desperation

3 ....Good News and Very Bad News

4 ....A Reluctant Bride

5 ....The New Boy

6 ....Hyenas

7 ....Bitterroot Camp

8 ....Suspicion

9 ....Grim Discovery

10 ....New Arrivals

11 ....Preparations

12 ....Detection and Disaster

13 ....The Pit

14 ....Aftermath

15 ....Into the High Mountains

16 ....Pursuit

17 ....Survival

18 ....Cornered

19 ....Blizzard

20 ....Capture

21 ....Decision

22 ....The Run to Missoula

23 ....Trial in Helena

24 ....A New Beginning

1

A Run for Freedom

Identical twins Rachel and Janie Lemon were ready for their run to Sheba. They weren't certain if they could pull it off or even if their plans made sense, but they knew they must try. To wait for their thirteenth birthday was unthinkable. They were determined not to end up like their sister Mary, even if it meant bruises and broken bones or even death on one of the dark trails that led down the hill.

After the Lemon household was asleep, they slipped out the back door and began their venture. Because the late November air was windy and cold, and they were uncertain how long they would be subjected to the elements, they dressed in layers, with heavy pants and heavy coats. They were thankful there was no snow on the ground. Generally at this time of year, the Montana prairie was blanketed in snow that didn't melt until spring. They crept to a position behind the back corner of the chapel where they could watch the security forces as they made their rounds.

Janie whispered, "The guard should come around in a few minutes…then he'll disappear over the ridge if he's on schedule."

"The minute he steps behind the ridge, we start running," said Rachel, "and we don't stop until we get to the rocks about halfway down the hill."

"I know, Rachel. The rocks were my idea."

Rachel nodded. "Just making sure we're on the

same page."

Janie pointed toward the west, "Look!"

The guard had made his appearance and was trudging across the horizon in the direction of the ridge.

"Wait until his head is out of sight," Rachel said softly. The instant he was no longer visible, they sprang to their feet and darted down the hill. The gravel and dirt under their feet crunched loudly, but they continued on, knowing if the guard or someone else heard them, there was little that could be done. When they reached the safety of the rock outcropping, they dove beneath a long overhang and scrambled deeper into the crevice below.

"Made it…I guess," said Rachel.

"We'll know in a minute," Janie said breathlessly.

When there were no sounds for several minutes, they looked at each other in relief. "I thought we sounded like a herd of elephants going down the hill," said Janie. "I was sure the guard must've heard us."

"He's probably dreaming about all the wives

he's going to get someday," said Rachel.

After another short interval they got to their feet

and began their circuitous path down the mountain.

When they reached the main road to Sheba they

decided to walk behind the trees about a hundred feet to

the side. If they stayed on the pavement, sooner or later

someone might come along and see them, and it would

be likely that whoever it was would belong to the Sheba

Temple. And their fears proved correct, for soon they

heard the low rumble of a large vehicle coming toward

them from the direction of Sheba Hill. They scurried

behind a thick oak tree and peered out to see the Sheba

Hill Security Service's large black SUV rolling slowly

down the hill. They pulled back behind the tree just as

a powerful spotlight shone through the branches above

them and on the ground on all sides of their hiding

place.

"So soon?" Janie whispered. "They're after us so soon?"

"Maybe not us," said Rachel. "Maybe someone else is trying to get away…or maybe it's just a regular security patrol."

"Do you think Mom and Dad woke up and turned us in?" Janie asked. "Would they do that?"

"Dad would. Mom would probably just worry about us being gone."

"Someone else in our house?"

"No one else cares about us except the boys, and they're too little to know what's going on. Dad's other wives wouldn't bother with us."

The SUV moved on toward Sheba; and the girls slipped from behind the oak and hiked carefully along the side of the road, ready at any moment to dart back into the woods should the guards return. "They might patrol like this every night," said Rachel. "The Prophet and the elders are afraid of their shadows these days."

**

At the edge of town Rachel reminded Janie that the temporary FBI offices were in the post office building and the best way to get there was to circle the business district while still among the trees and come out on the opposite side of town.

"The FBI office won't be open," Janie said.

"No, but the post office will. We can curl up inside in a corner somewhere until morning and then go upstairs."

As they exited the woods a few hundred feet from the post office, they were startled by the sudden reappearance of the SUV. It had reached the halfway point around the traffic circle and was now headed back toward Sheba Hill. Its spotlight was off, but its headlights lit the road and the surrounding area like the eyes of a huge black dragon. Without exchanging a word, the girls whirled around and raced back under cover. This time they remained concealed for fear the guards would activate the spotlight and search the woods.

"Don't stick your head out!" Rachel warned.

"Don't worry, I won't," said Janie.

After the sound of the SUV's engine faded in the distance, they stepped out and began to make their way toward the post office. The inside lights were on and the glass double doors were unlocked. Rachel entered first and Janie followed, after looking around to make certain no one was watching. They moved deeper into the building, hesitating in front of the notice board that contained federal information and photographs of wanted criminals.

"J.J. Flack's picture should be up there," said Janie.

"And all the elders, too," said Rachel.

A few feet beyond the board, Rachel stopped abruptly and said, "Wait a minute! What was that in the right-hand corner—above the mail fraud guy?"

They focused on the small white announcement:

The temporary offices of the Federal Bureau of Investigation have been closed. All operations have been transferred to Helena.

"Oh, no!" said Janie. "We're too late."

Rachel shook her head. "But we're not defeated. There are other outsiders here in town. Someone will help us. You'll see in the morning. We'll find the right people and we'll get away, Janie. I promise you we will."

"A foolish promise, dear," said a deep voice behind them. They turned to see Elder Biggars, their fat, red-faced, forty-eight-year-old prospective husband grinning triumphantly at them. "Hello, ladies."

"We're not ladies," said Rachel defiantly. "We're twelve-year-old girls."

"You'll soon be thirteen," Elder Biggars said with a cold smile.

2

Act of Desperation

"Our time's running out," said Janie. "We'll be thirteen in two months. We've got to try something else."

"They've tripled the guards on the roads and trails down to Sheba," said Rachel.

She was sitting on a cane-back chair in front of their dressing mirror. Janie was standing behind her brushing her sister's long blonde hair. Janie's hair was an identical color and also very long. Rachel was dressed in a gray flannel gown tied at the neck, and Janie was wearing flannel pajamas decorated with hundreds of little red hearts.

"We need to get smaller," said Janie, "like Alice in Wonderland. We need a little bottle that says DRINK ME on it. If we were ten inches high, we could slip past the temple guards and make it to Sheba."

"If the dogs, cats, or goats don't eat us."

They both laughed.

Rachel said, "We don't have much time left. We don't want to end up as two of Elder Biggars' wives. The thought of staring at that ghoul for the rest of our lives makes me ill."

Janie grimaced. "I wish we could escape down Alice's rabbit hole."

"I've got an idea," said Rachel. "It's not a permanent solution, but it might cause them to postpone the wedding. Any extra time would help."

They left the house and headed for the gazebo

next to the old covered well. It was a favorite spot for

them, and they'd played, talked, and giggled there since

they were toddlers. When Rachel explained her plan,

Janie said, "It might work. No, I *know* it'll work. How

about tonight?"

"Why not?" said Rachel.

**

They were thankful the floodlights were

concentrated toward the center of the compound and the

quarter moon was not bright enough to light the outer

areas, but even in the darkness they could see the

outline form of a temple guard patrolling about a

hundred yards from their position. They waited until he

disappeared over the ridge, and then they moved out to

begin their work. Rachel carried a small paper bag, and

Janie carried a gallon milk jug filled with a clear liquid.

Hank Biggars' unfinished new home stood on a

small rise close behind his barn, not too far from his

present house. The new structure was a three-level

mansion, necessary to accommodate the elder's

growing family—children and wives.

The milk jug Janie was carrying contained

kerosene, and she began to soak the naked studs along

the darkest side of the structure. When Janie completed

her task, Rachel stepped forward and removed two

items from her paper bag: a box of kitchen matches and

a handheld digging tool. "Let's dig the hole first,"

Rachel said, "and then light the kerosene. That way

we'll be ready to bury the stuff quickly."

They moved back to a spot under a large ash

tree where they knelt while Rachel dug and Janie

scooped the dirt into a mound that could be readily

shoved back into the hole. Then they gathered a small

pile of leaves so they could camouflage the area when

they were through. Next, they crept back to the

building site and Rachel struck a match and touched off

the kerosene. The flames leapt toward the sky and the

girls recoiled in surprise. They hadn't expected such an eruption and they looked at each other in shock.

"Run!" shouted Janie. The fire was illuminating her frightened face, and she was already moving as she spoke. Rachel followed close behind, her long blonde hair blowing in the wind; and when they reached the hole to bury the evidence, they took only a few seconds to dump the milk jug, matches, and trowel and to kick in the dirt and cover everything with leaves. They raced home, slipped in the back door, and were in their room, breathing heavily, when they heard the first shouts coming from the outer perimeter where Elder Biggars' new house stood. They grinned at each other in satisfaction, and Rachel said, "Well, that should slow the old fool down."

**

What they didn't know at the time was that the fire had escalated far beyond what they had intended. A burning ember from the construction site had set the roof of the barn on fire; and shortly thereafter an ember from the barn had blown onto the roof of Elder Biggars' present house. All three buildings were soon ablaze. Fortunately, no one was hurt in any of the three fires, and Rachel and Janie were greatly relieved. "What if someone had died?" said Rachel. "One of the children or one of Elder Biggars' wives?"

"We would never have forgiven ourselves," said Janie. "We would have felt guilty for the rest of our lives."

Rachel said, "Unless Hank Biggars himself had been burned up. That wouldn't have been so bad."

"No," Janie objected. "We didn't want that either. We're not killers, Rachel."

"I know. I'm only joking. But the thought of our future husband roasting is sort of pleasant, wouldn't you agree?"

"Well, a little pleasant."

**

Two fire trucks raced up the hill from the town of Sheba, but they were too late to be effective, and soon after their arrival they were reduced to pouring water on three heaps of smoldering ruins.

The twins watched the action from the safety of the large crowd that had gathered behind the fire lines. Elder Biggars, the Prophet J.J. Flack, and several other elders and deacons stood in front of the girls, talking about the fire and about how it would affect Biggars' immediate plans.

"Four to six months and I'll be back on track," said Biggars.

The other men waited for the Prophet to respond. They obviously had no wish to make a comment that would be stepped on or overruled by their leader. The twins' father Seth Lemon was among the men, and Rachel and Janie stared at his back, aware that he was no different from the others; and they suspected he was worse. They were fairly certain he was the one who had reported them missing the night they were

captured on their run to Sheba.

The Prophet cleared his throat, and all of the

men turned toward him anxiously. His long iron-gray

hair shone in the dying firelight, and his hooded eyes

were filled with purpose and insight. "This fire may be

a sign from God," he said. "I believe I'm now

receiving new messages, new plans, new revelations."

"Like what?" Biggars asked hesitantly. The

suspicion in his voice revealed he was aware that

whenever the Prophet began to receive information

directly from God, someone in the vicinity was going to

come out on the short end of the stick.

3

Good News and Very Bad News

The morning sky over Sheba Hill was streaked with red and orange from the rising sun, and there was still a residue of gray smoke in the air from the fires the night before. The twins stepped off their front porch, buttoned their coats, and headed for the temple to attend early morning chapel. They were required to attend one of the Sunday services, and they always chose the earliest so they would be free for the rest of the day.

"No one said a word about arson," Janie said.

"They wouldn't admit it, even if they suspected," said Rachel. "Our people are above such crimes. Arson is for the outside world."

"But the fire department—"

"They're all church members. They'll say what the Prophet wants them to say. Anyway, there may not be any evidence. That was a hot, hot fire. Nothing left."

"The kerosene?"

"Gone—no smell, nothing."

"Good, let's hope so."

They were wearing matching beige cloth coats, matching long dark blue dresses, and even their shoes were identical. They hated dressing this way. They preferred to express their individuality, but the Prophet insisted that when attending public affairs, they appear as a team, a unit, a double image. He explained that they symbolized a double portion—and God demanded double portions.

**

The Prophet's full name was John Joseph Flack, son of John Joseph Flack, and grandson of John Joseph Flack. The Sheba Hill Fellowship was an offshoot of an offshoot of the Latter Day Saints. When the Mormons opted for respectability by discontinuing polygamy, a small group chose to ignore such restrictions and moved their operation to South Dakota. And some years later when the South Dakota group decided to minimize polygamy (while not outlawing it), the original J.J. Flack herded his people into the Montana wilderness with the comment that God doesn't change, and therefore neither should the practices and beliefs of God's people change. In Montana they established the town of Sheba, and on the highest point in the area, they built the Sheba Hill Temple. The first two J.J. Flacks were gone, and all power was now concentrated in the hands of John Joseph III who ran the sect as if it were his own private kingdom—which

in fact it was.

In chapel he wore a long purple robe and stood

on an extremely high dais as he addressed his subjects.

"Please come to order, my dear friends."

Rachel and Janie sat with their three little

brothers (each from a different mother) sandwiched

between them. The boys were five, seven, and nine;

and the instruction to come to order did not change their

behavior. All three were fidgeting, shoving, and

kicking, and it didn't appear Moses himself could settle

them down.

"Young men!" the Prophet said sharply.

"Please sit still and behave or we will think of some

creative punishment for you after chapel."

The boys ceased their activity at once. Even at

their age, they knew that punishment on Sheba Hill

could be very severe indeed, and they wanted no part of

it.

**

Toward the end of his message the Prophet

announced a decision that changed everything. At first

the girls thought they were receiving good news, for the

Prophet decreed that because of the fire, the marriage of

the Lemon twins to Elder Biggars would not take place.

The girls were overjoyed, and they nudged one another

in relief. Their scheme had worked.

Biggars didn't like the news one bit, and against

all Sheba Hill protocol he leapt to his feet in protest.

"What's this?" he stammered. "What's this all about?"

His jowly round face was scarlet with anxiety and fury,

and he was breaking the primary commandment of the

Sheba Hill society: never question the Prophet. He was

sovereign and no dissent of any kind was tolerated.

"Settle down, brother," the Prophet said

smoothly. "God has appeared to me personally and

made it clear that—"

"But, sir…there's no need to—" He now

realized he was going too far, and he looked around to see who was watching and listening.

The Prophet hurriedly dismissed the congregation and took Biggars by the arm and led him to a small alcove off the main auditorium.

After shooing their little brothers out the front door, Rachel and Janie crept back inside the temple to see if they could overhear what Biggars and the Prophet were talking about. The two men's voices were muffled, and the girls knew if they were to understand what was being said, they needed to make it to a position behind the marble pillar that stood about ten feet from the alcove. They measured each step carefully, halting when there was a pause in the men's conversation and creeping forward again when the men resumed talking. At the pillar, Rachel looked into her sister's bright green eyes and indicated with a nod that they should both squeeze into the space between the pillar and the wall.

"God makes the final decisions in these matters," said the Prophet.

"Yes, yes, I know. But why is it necessary to cancel—"

"Because God has told me the Lemon girls are to be my wives."

"No, wait," Biggars stammered. "You got Mary, and now you want her sisters. That's not fair. I've always been loyal—a good soldier and I deserve—"

"Yes, you're a good soldier, and I need you and count on you. You're my most trusted aide. But God makes these choices, not me."

Biggars lowered his head submissively. "I know that. But it hurts, and it doesn't seem right."

"I'll make it up to you."

The Elder assented, but his voice was weak and unhappy.

The twins stared at each other in astonishment.

The fire had not saved them after all. It had given the

Prophet the excuse he needed to claim them as his own.

Janie gasped at the thought, and Rachel reached out and

covered her sister's mouth with her hand. But the men

had heard the sound, and they stopped their

conversation abruptly. They remained silent for several

long moments, and then Biggars said, "What was that?"

"Hold on," the Prophet said, "let's see."

The girls burrowed into their nook, folding into

each other's arms so they could slip deeper into the

narrow space behind the pillar.

The men began to search the chapel to see if

anyone was present. They examined the aisles toward

the back entrance and then turned to walk toward the

front near the altar. Seeing nothing, they grunted with

satisfaction. "No one," said the Prophet.

The girls held their breath; and Janie reached

out and tucked the hem of her dress under her leg. She

motioned for Rachel to do the same, for the blue

material from their long dresses was extending beyond

the pillar and out onto the hardwood floor.

The men moved down the aisle in the direction

of the rear exit, and as they passed the pillar their faces

came into view. The Prophet's expression was one of

control and self-satisfaction, but Hank Biggars' face

was contorted with rage, and his eyes were filled with

hate.

When they were alone, the twins eased out of

their hiding place and went out through the side door

behind the dais. They ran to the gazebo, and when they

were seated on the familiar safe bench, they turned to

each other in dismay. "What now?" asked Rachel.

"I don't know," said Janie, "but I know one

thing for sure. We are not going to end up like Mary."

"We've got to get away," said Rachel, "get to

Sheba, get some help."

They were startled by a sound at the base of the

gazebo, about five feet below where they were sitting.

They jumped up at the same time and saw a boy disappearing into the nearby woods. He had apparently been sitting on the grass with his back against the latticework. He was carrying a book in his hand.

"Do you think he heard us?" asked Janie.

"How could he help but hear."

"Do you think he'll tell?"

Rachel shrugged. "Probably. They're all brainwashed in this place."

"Did you recognize him?"

"I think it was the new boy Justin—the one who came in with his aunt a couple of months ago."

"Maybe they haven't had time to brainwash him yet."

"I guess we'll find out."

4

A Reluctant Bride

One week after her thirteenth birthday, the twins'
older sister Mary Lemon had become the tenth
wife of J.J. Flack, the Prophet of Sheba Hill, a
hatchet-faced, black-eyed, Doberman pinscher of a
man in his fifties. Some years earlier, he had
decreed she was to be the wife of Elder Hank
Biggars, his trusted aide-de-camp; but the Prophet
watched her as she developed, and when it became

obvious she was going to blossom into an

extraordinary beauty, he claimed her for himself.

Elder Biggars didn't like it, but there was nothing

he could do because the Prophet ruled the Sheba

Hill Temple with an iron fist.

Rachel and Janie Lemon were eleven at the

time, and they were told that one day they would

replace their sister in Hank Biggars' harem. They were

supposed to look forward to their thirteenth birthday

when they would step in as his sixth and seventh, or

maybe his eighth and ninth wives, depending on who

caught his fancy in the interim. He was fat, in his mid-

forties, arrogant, and cruel; and to say Rachel and Janie

were not eagerly anticipating the day when they would

join his family, would be the understatement of the

century.

Mary didn't live up to the expectations of her

bridegroom, for almost immediately after her wedding,

she descended into a physical, spiritual, emotional, and

mental funk that turned her into a zombie in a polyester

housecoat. Her decline was astonishing to see, and by

the time she reached her fourteenth birthday, everyone

in the compound knew it was unlikely she would live to

see fifteen. Rachel and Janie were devastated. They

loved their older sister and they begged their mother

and father to help Mary, to save her. But Seth and

Esther Lemon's response was to go to the Prophet and

ask him what he thought about Mary's deterioration.

He assured them she was fine and healthy and was

merely going through a stage that would soon disappear

as she recognized God's working in her life. Seth and

Esther were satisfied with his answer, as they were with

every answer the Prophet gave them. They belonged to

him, body and soul, and for them to question his

judgment or his decisions was inconceivable.

Rachel and Janie were considerably less

impressed. They suspected that the only god the

Prophet worshipped was himself—but they were too

young to fight him, too young to contest his will, too young to help Mary. "Maybe we should go back to Mother and Father," Janie said, "try to convince them to do something."

Rachel shook her head. "Mother is dominated by Father, and he's not going to make any waves. He likes things the way they are."

"He doesn't want Mary to suffer."

"That's not what I mean….Father is forty-four years old. He has four wives and he wants more. If he causes trouble he'll move down on the waiting list, and he knows that."

"Then Mother—"

"Mother doesn't think for herself anymore. We both know that. No, it's up to us to help Mary. We'll have to come up with a plan."

"What kind of a plan, Rachel?"

"I don't know."

But before they could organize their ideas or

even think the matter through clearly, Mary died, and the plan to save her became meaningless. The Prophet said it was a stroke, but the twins knew better. Except in very rare instances, children don't get strokes. Mary had given up. She'd stared into the future and had seen no hope, no love, and no reason to continue living.

Rachel and Janie Lemon were determined they would not share the same fate.

**

At Mary's funeral Elder Hank Biggars, their betrothed, tried to comfort the girls by assuring them Mary was in a better place. But all he succeeded in doing was to turn their stomachs and to cause Janie to agree there was little doubt their sister was in a better place. Biggars was too pompous and self-absorbed to pick up on the broader meaning in Janie's comment, even when she muttered under her breath that it wouldn't be hard to find a better place than Sheba Hill, Montana.

"Yes, yes," he said, "a better place." As he

spoke, his greedy pig's eyes carefully evaluated the

twins, and it was obvious he was thinking about the day

when they would become his brides.

Rachel and Janie exchanged glances and shared

a moment of silent determination. Such a marriage

would never take place, not if they could prevent it.

"I despise him," said Janie, after Biggars

departed.

"He's an easy man to despise," Rachel said.

**

The twins did their best to avoid Elder Biggars

and the Prophet during the next year, but they were not

entirely successful. On many occasions they felt both

men watching them, studying them. The girls knew as

they approached their thirteenth birthday, they were

emerging, changing, growing into graceful young

women—still awkward, but with unlimited promise.

And they were certain their keepers knew also.

Fortunately, Biggars and the Prophet couldn't give undivided attention to the twins' development, for this was a difficult period for the church. The sect was buffeted by the authorities, by rejected relatives who wanted their family members back, and by former church members who had left the movement and were now attacking from the outside. The leaders couldn't breathe; and they spent most of their waking hours hiding the truth about their beliefs from those who would like to do harm to the organization.

Rachel and Janie desperately wished to escape from the Sheba Hill Temple, to run away, to find refuge. The problem was they didn't know how. They thought they might go into the town of Sheba to see if any of the newcomers would help them; but there were now new rules against leaving the compound. Before the trouble with the outsiders, all of the children, teenagers, and young adults had constant access to Sheba. After all, the town was essentially an extension of the Sheba Hill congregation. Church members owned most of the businesses and ran most of the institutions. There was no risk of what the leaders called negative influence, because there were few residents or visitors who didn't subscribe to the doctrines of the Sheba Hill Temple. But with the onset of the trouble, this began to change. The FBI was in town looking for witnesses to crimes against minors, and everyone knew it; and the girls thought if only they could steal away from the compound and make it to the FBI's temporary office, they would be safe. They would never have to sit across the breakfast table from Elder Biggars and listen to him expound on why they were so lucky to be a part of his family. The very thought caused them to double and redouble their planning.

And yet, the more they concentrated and schemed, the less practical their ideas seemed. The temple guards were everywhere—especially at night;

and every exit from the compound was covered. The

Prophet explained he was protecting his flock from the

harassment of outsiders, so all could focus on the things

of God and not on the things of the world. But the

twins knew that while he certainly didn't want to let

outsiders in, he was also deathly afraid of letting rebels

out.

"We can't get out and we can't stay here," said

Rachel, "not with our wedding coming up in less than

four months." Her bottle-green eyes were filled with

frustration and anger, and she hurled a schoolbook

against the bedroom wall, causing a small figurine to

fall from the shelf. It didn't break, and she put it back

in place.

"What can we do?" asked Janie. Her tear-filled

eyes were lighter than her sister's, a brighter green, like

undiluted antifreeze. Everyone knew the surest way to

tell the girls apart was to look at their eyes. But those

who knew them best also knew another way to identify

them was to see who had taken the lead, for Rachel was the more aggressive of the two.

"Don't cry, Janie," said Rachel, "we'll come up with something. I've been working on an idea."

"What?"

And they began to plan their night run to Sheba.

5

The New Boy

Twelve-year-old Justin Patrick missed his

father, his uncle, and Alaska. He missed the treks the

three of them made into the back country; and he

missed the rescues his father organized to save the lives

of stranded climbers, skiers, and downed pilots. He

missed the survival lessons, the rugged Alaskan

wilderness, and the camaraderie he shared with the two

men in his family. His aunt was now the only family he

had left. The landslide had taken his father and his uncle, and his mother had died when he was an infant.

Aunt Ruby was not blood family. She was Uncle Garth's wife and related to Justin only by marriage. While Uncle Garth lived, she seemed as solid and stable as her husband; but after his death she began a long decline culminating in her leaving Alaska for Montana and the Sheba Hill congregation.

Justin was devastated by her decision. After he and his aunt had moved into a small home in the Sheba Hill compound, he went to her and said, "How can we be part of this?"

"These are good people," she said.

He shook his head.

"The Prophet loves us," she said.

Justin scowled. "He loves himself and young girls."

"Try to believe in the Prophet," she said. "He has your best interests in mind."

Justin closed his eyes in disgust. "I don't believe in him, Aunt Ruby, and I never will." His expression was intense, and his pale blue eyes were defiant. "As soon as I'm able, I'm going to get out of this place."

"Don't be ridiculous, Justin. Where would you go? Who would you go to? I'm all you have—me and our new family here at Sheba Hill."

"And your new husband and his other wives?"

"Elder Tate is a wonderful man, and I'm fortunate he wants me for his wife."

Justin shook his head. "One of his wives, you mean. If Uncle Garth knew what you're doing, he'd crawl out of his grave and come drag you away from here."

"That's not funny, Justin."

"I'm not trying to be funny."

**

After his aunt married Elder Tate, Justin tried to

stay away from the Tate household as much as possible.

He asked if he could continue to live in the small

cottage he and Ruby had previously occupied, but the

Prophet said Justin was too young to live alone; and

besides, he needed the warmth of a family unit.

Family unit? The Tate ménage was more like a

zoo, with children running everywhere and wives in

cages of their own construction. Justin's only relief

was to find ways to spend as much time by himself as

he could. He often got up at first light and didn't return

to the house until after dark. Today was no exception.

He'd snuck out before dawn, intending to skip chapel if

he could get away with it. He went for a long walk

along the outer edges of the compound, observing the

temple guards for future reference. And then he took

the wilderness survival book, written by his father, to

the gazebo by the old covered well. He sat down on the

grass with his back against the latticework and began to

read. It was a cold late fall morning, and he shivered a

bit; but cold or not, it was better than the Tate house and its monstrous hypocrisies.

He heard the Lemon twins run into the gazebo above him, heard their sighs and exclamations of dismay, and then heard Janie say, "…We are not going to end up like Mary" and heard Rachel's response, "We've got to get away, get to Sheba for some help." He wasn't quite sure what they meant, but he had his suspicions. He knew the twins were approaching their thirteenth birthday and when the date arrived they would be given in marriage to one of the arrogant old men—and he was virtually certain the girls recoiled at such a union. He was tempted to stand up, show himself and tell them he understood and was on their side. But he chose not to do so. He could have misinterpreted their conversation, and even if he was assessing the situation correctly, his sudden appearance might frighten them and cause them distress. He rose to his feet and strode quickly to the woods, hoping they had not noticed him.

**

At dinner Sunday evening (always an unappealing event, with Elder Tate presiding at a table of browbeaten wives and children), Justin made it a point to find out all he could about the Lemon twins. The answers were positive, and the elder made it clear the girls were anxiously awaiting their marriage to one of the elders or deacons of the Sheba Hill Temple. Tate wasn't certain who the bridegroom would be since the Prophet had cancelled the girls' marriage to Hank Biggars; but he knew the Prophet would make a wise and appropriate choice.

Justin stared at his new uncle and concluded that the odious old man could not conceive of a situation where young girls would not be delighted with marriage to a prominent leader in the Sheba Hill congregation.

"Why all the questions?" asked Aunt Ruby.

"I'm just trying to make friends," Justin said.

She nodded. "Good, good. It's time you came out of your shell."

Elder Tate tightened his lips and said, "Keep in mind that those two young women will soon be dutiful wives. Don't establish any improper relationships."

Justin nearly gagged on his food. Improper? Tate was warning *him* about being improper? Amazing. "Young women?" he said. "I thought they were still little girls."

"What?" Tate said, straining to hear.

"Nothing," said Justin.

**

At school the next morning he came face to face with the Lemon twins on the landing of the main staircase. They all paused and stared at one another, but no one spoke. Justin considered blurting out that he sympathized with them, but he held his tongue. There were other children passing on both sides, and he didn't want to be overheard. And he still didn't fully comprehend what the twins' attitudes were. He wanted

allies, but he didn't want to open a can of worms

because of an incorrect assessment of the situation.

Rachel broke the ice and said, "Hi,"

"The gazebo is nice, isn't it?" said Janie.

"Yes, I like to go there and read."

The girls exchanged glances, and Rachel said,

"We saw you there yesterday. Were you reading

something by the Prophet?"

Justin took a breath. "I don't read books by the

Prophet."

6

Hyenas

In the presence of the assembled elders, the

Prophet lavishly praised Seth Lemon for his loyalty to

God. "You will be rewarded for your service, both here

and in the world to come."

Seth lowered his head and basked in his leader's

approbation. He still felt a degree of residual guilt for

calling security on the night he discovered his twin

daughters were not in the house and that many of their

significant belongings were gone. But his guilt was fast

disappearing in the glow of the Prophet's words. Seth's

wife Esther had suggested they handle the situation

themselves and there was no need to involve the Sheba

Hill authorities. She and Seth could go out and find the

girls, lecture them on their foolishness in trying to leave

the compound, and bring them home safely and quietly

with no one the wiser. But he had balked. What if the

Prophet found out and interpreted their actions as

disloyalty. That would spoil everything; and he would

be shunned, degraded. And now he knew he'd done the

right thing, for as the Prophet spoke, the intent of his

words was becoming increasingly clear.

"As most of you know, we have an opening for

a new elder, and I can't think of a better candidate than

Brother Seth Lemon."

Seth reddened. It was what he had dreamed

about for the past ten years. His power and authority

would skyrocket, and he would no longer be limited in

the number of young wives he could acquire. And because the Prophet himself had made the proposal, the vote would be a mere formality. None of the current elders would dare oppose a candidate put forth personally by the Prophet. Seth nodded humbly, acknowledging the honor; and after a brief moment of concern about what might now happen to his twin daughters, he continued to daydream about his bright future.

Elder Hank Biggars shifted his bulk on the chapel's wooden bench and made a short, positive comment regarding Seth's proposed elevation. Biggars then moved on to what was really on his mind. With his jaw set and his eyes narrowed, he said, "Maybe the girls will attempt another run one of these days because their marriage to me was so abruptly cancelled. Young women don't appreciate having their wedding plans tampered with." He was about to make an additional comment regarding the Prophet's decision to step in as the girls' new bridegroom, but a glance at his leader's

stern expression convinced him to remain silent about

the matter. As far as he knew, only he and the Prophet

were aware of the new arrangement.

The other men in the group reacted to Biggars'

remarks with astonished smiles and restrained snickers.

To hear that the twins might attempt another escape

from the compound because of their terrible

disappointment in losing the rotund Hank Biggars was

almost too ludicrous to consider. Elder Tate put his

hand on Biggars' shoulder. "An interesting thought,

brother. But maybe the girls can survive the blow and

find some way to live with their loss."

The Prophet regained the group's attention by

tapping on the lectern with his fingers. "Our primary

concern today is to prevent another escape attempt by

the Lemon girls or by anyone else so inclined. But

more than that, we must recapture the loyalty of these

young people…so they become solid, productive

members of our community. With this in mind I've

spoken to God about this situation, and He has

instructed me to send the girls along with Elder Riggs'

rebellious wife to Bitterroot Camp for the winter. By

the time Spring arrives they should all be thoroughly

submissive. When they return to the compound, I'm

certain we'll be delighted with their metamorphosis."

"Won't they try to leave the camp?" asked Hank

Biggars.

The Prophet smiled. "Elder Mobly and his

wives have established some effective security

procedures. Besides, as those of you who helped me set

up the retraining camp know, it stands deep in the

Bitterroots, miles from the nearest neighbor. It would

be an impossible trek to get out—especially in sub-zero

weather. Enough to discourage even the hardiest

rebels."

Seth Lemon took a deep breath and asked,

"What kind of retraining do we do there? What's our

success rate? Do we have examples…here at the compound?"

"Too new," said the Prophet. "Right now we're still learning. There have been some early failures, I'll admit, but we've changed some things and soon we'll be on the right track?"

"Failures?" said Seth, "What kind of failures?"

"Don't worry Elder Lemon, we're not running a concentration camp."

Seth blushed at the use of his prospective title. "I didn't mean to question—"

The Prophet held up his hand. "I know. Just keep in mind that we follow God's lead in these matters, and what I carelessly referred to as failures are really part of God's overall plan."

Elder Tate said, "I believe my new stepson Justin Patrick should also be sent to Bitterroot. He tries to hide it, but he's filled with antagonism and disrespect. I don't believe he's fully recovered from the death of his father. He could develop into a problem if we don't act now. If anyone needs retraining, it's Justin."

"So be it," said the Prophet.

7

Bitterroot Camp

After the long drive across the prairie and

through the Northern Rocky Mountain passes, the van

left I-90 at Missoula and turned south on Route 93

through the Bitterroot Valley. To the west stood

Trapper Peak, the highest point in the Bitterroots, and

farther south was Lost Trail Pass where Lewis and

Clark crossed the mountains in 1805 on their way back

from the Snake River. After about an hour and a half,

the van left the highway and headed west toward the Idaho border on a series of gravel and dirt roads upward into the range that formed Montana's western spine.

The driver and the security guard occupied the front seats and were carrying on a running lamentation regarding the rough roads and the constant bumping. Rachel and Janie Lemon, Justin Patrick, and Mrs. Riggs, the disenchanted Sheba Hill wife, sat in the back. Mrs. Riggs did little but stare mournfully out the window, but Justin and the girls were engaged in an animated conversation.

Janie said, "You mean you think you could walk out of this place?"

Justin nodded. "Of course I could." He tapped the cover of his father's survival book. My dad taught me a hundred ways to live in the woods. And I could take you girls with me, too."

"In the winter?" asked Rachel.

"Winter, spring, summer, or fall. He taught me

everything."

Mrs. Riggs turned from the window and said, "Why don't you stop giving these girls false hope. You're not going anywhere, and you're not taking them anywhere."

"I could take you, too," Justin said carefully. He lowered his voice. "Wouldn't you like to get away, Mrs. Riggs?"

"Get away? To where? Who would want us? Who would take us in?"

"The authorities," said Justin, "to start with. Then who knows? We could all start new lives."

"My life is over," she said. "Leave me alone."

**

Bitterroot Camp stood at the end of a long, winding gravel road about fifteen miles from the Idaho border. The camp consisted of one sprawling two-story building and three smaller one-story buildings, two on the south side of the main structure and one in the rear.

Elder Mobly and two of his four wives met the van under the portico. He explained that his other two wives were busy in the kitchen and would introduce themselves when everyone went inside. He was a very tall, whippet thin man, and he seemed to be trying his best to appear grandfatherly and gracious.

Justin and the girls were still filled with excitement about the idea of escaping from the clutches of the Sheba Hill Temple, and Mobly apparently mistook their exuberance for submissiveness and willingness to change. He smiled warmly.

"Good, good," he said. "We're off to a good start. We'll have a fine winter."

Mrs. Riggs remained inside the van and sat motionless, without expression. Her eyes were red and her face tearstained, and she gave no indication she was aware the van had come to a stop. The driver and the guard began to pull the luggage through the van's rear door, and the driver spoke to Mrs. Riggs. "Please get out.”

She shook her head.

“If you don’t get out, we’ll have to carry you. That wouldn’t be a very good beginning.”

“Beginning to what?” she said. “My so-called retraining, my brainwashing? I assure you it’s not going to work with me. Maybe with these children, but not with me.” But while she was speaking, she seemed to realize the futility of physical resistance and she stepped down from the van and went to stand by the front door.

**

Justin’s high spirits were crushed on his second day in camp when Elder Mobly stuck out his long bony hand and said, “Please give me that book.”

“Why?” said Justin.

“Because it’s distracting you from our lessons.”

They were in a small brightly-lit training room on the second floor of the main building. Justin was sitting behind Rachel, and while Elder Mobly had been writing maxims from the Prophet on the blackboard, Justin had been sneaking peaks at his survival guide. He had just begun to review the section on building shelters when Mobly whirled about, took a long step past Rachel, and snatched the book away.

"I'm not distracted," said Justin. "I was listening."

"Listening perhaps, but not concentrating," said Mobly.

Mrs. Riggs, who had been staring blankly at the wall during most of the session, looked up at the elder and said, "Why don't you leave the boy alone? Give him his book back and stop harassing him."

"Well, good morning, Mrs. Riggs," said Mobly, "it's nice to hear from you. I thought you were in another country."

"No, I'm here," she said. "Unfortunately. But I assure you I'm not listening to the garbage you're spewing about J.J. Flack."

Mobly's eyes narrowed. "Be very careful what you say, Mrs. Riggs."

She laughed somewhat hysterically and said, "For seven years I lived with Elder Riggs, the cruelest, most hateful man in Montana, and you think I'm afraid of a pitiful scarecrow like you."

Justin said, "If you give me back my book, I promise to put it away and not take it out again during training classes."

Mobly thought for a moment and then returned the book. "Okay, Justin, I'll take you at your word."

Justin was pleased that at no point had the elder looked at the book's title. He resolved that in the future he would leave it in his room and not give his jailers the slightest hint regarding what he was planning.

8

Suspicion

The van driver and the guard entered through the front door, stomping their feet and complaining about the snow. "At least a foot thick," said the guard. "It was tough going all the way."

Their arms were laden with supplies, and they headed for the kitchen where Rachel, Janie and Justin sat eating their dinner. Two of Elder Mobly's wives were busy at the counter and both rushed to help the men with their bags and packages.

Rachel looked at her watch, whispered something to her sister and Justin, and then said loudly, "Where's Mrs. Riggs?"

There was no immediate answer from either of the men; and then the guard, after disposing of his portion of the supplies, removed his coat and said slowly, "Missoula—we took her to Missoula…She'll be going to Texas. The Prophet has a Temple in the Hill Country near Austin. Mrs. Riggs wanted a fresh start."

The older of the two wives, a woman in her forties, turned from the cabinet she was restocking. She was frail and nervous, and she wiped her hands on her apron. "How about some nice peach cobbler, children? Maybe with some ice cream?"

Rachel looked at her and wondered why the woman was so uncomfortable. "No, thank you," she said. And Janie and Justin said no as well.

The younger wife, a girl of fifteen or sixteen with a vacant expression said, "The cobbler's good. You kids should try some."

Rachel thought it seemed inappropriate for the girl to call them "kids" when she was no more than a kid herself. But maybe life here in the Bitterroot Mountains with Elder Mobly and his other three wives had caused her to grow up faster than she might have under other circumstances.

When the driver and the guard departed, Janie whispered to Justin and Rachel, "Why are the driver and the guard still here? Why didn't they go back to Sheba Hill?"

"I don't know, but I have my suspicions," said Rachel. She looked at her watch again. "They didn't have time to take Mrs. Riggs to Missoula. They're lying."

"Do you think they hurt her?" asked Janie.

Justin whispered, "Or worse, maybe. I watched

when they left. They used the old road behind the complex. It might join the highway somewhere later on, but I don't think so. I think it heads higher…deeper into the mountains."

Janie started, "But why—"

Rachel put her hand on her sister's arm. "Don't you see? They must've decided Mrs. Riggs was untrainable. They don't want her on the loose, telling the truth about the Prophet and his madhouse. Bad publicity and maybe jail time for the leaders….I think they took her on a one-way trip into the wilderness and disposed of her."

Janie gasped. "You mean killed her?" She'd spoken a bit louder than she'd intended and both wives looked over sharply.

"What're you kids talking about so seriously?" said the frail, older wife. "There's no need for secrets around here." She attempted a smile, but only her mouth was involved, and her eyes remained empty and devoid of warmth. "After all, we're one big family here, and we share everything."

Justin snickered. "Yes, you certainly do that."

**

"Two thoughts," said Rachel when they were in their classroom waiting for Elder Mobly to conduct their evening sessions. "One, we'd better start pretending we're getting the message, coming around. If we don't, Mobly might call the Prophet and we'll find out for sure what happened to Mrs. Riggs, and I don't think we'll like it. Two, we need to figure out some way to get out of this place."

Janie frowned. "But we're in the Bitterroot Mountains, miles from anywhere. I didn't see any houses on the way up here, and I doubt there's anything above us either."

"Maybe we could steal one of their cars or the van," said Rachel.

"Do either of you know how to drive?" Justin

asked.

Both shook their heads.

"Neither do I," he said. "So we walk out."

Rachel said, "It'd be better to die out there than to have to listen to any more of the Sheba Hill loyalty crud we're hearing. Every time Mobly opens his mouth I want to smash him with an iron frying pan."

"We won't die," Justin said, "not if we prepare properly. Remember, I told you I'm trained in this sort of thing. We could load up our rooms with the necessities—I can tell you what we need. We can do it little by little. I'm from Alaska, remember. My father and my uncle were survivalists. They rescued lost climbers, skiers, pilots—you name it—and they taught me a lot of what they knew. If we prepare right, we won't die. It'll be hard going if we're forced up into the higher Bitterroots, but I promise you, we'll survive."

"Couldn't we go down?" Janie asked.

"I don't think so. That's the first direction they'll search. They'd be on us in no time, and –"

Elder Mobly strode into the room, his long face serious and filled with purpose. "Okay, children, let's get down to business. We've got a lot to cover."

"Where's Mrs. Riggs?" asked Justin.

"She wanted to go to the Texas compound, so we accommodated her," he said.

No one argued with him, and Rachel smiled and said, "Let's get into our lessons. I think we're starting to get the point."

Mobly said, "Good, good. I had hopes for all of you. I told them you'd come around. Perhaps I was correct."

9

Grim Discovery

Rachel and Janie shared a double bed in a small sparsely furnished room on the second floor. The bed was no problem because the girls had always slept together. In fact, since the day they were born, they had not spent a single night in separate beds. Tonight Justin had plopped on their bed and the girls were sprawled on the floor looking up at him. He lay on his stomach with his head hanging over the side.

"Is there any way to find out for sure what happened to Mrs. Riggs?" asked Janie.

"I think so," said Justin. "I'm going to sneak out later and see if I can track them—see where they went. But I might not be able to because of the fresh snow. My hope is the snow stopped before they got underway.

"Will you be okay?" asked Rachel. "Won't you get lost?"

He laughed. "One time my father flew my uncle and me to a spot ninety miles from Anchorage and told us to find our way home. We made it, and we only had a knife and some fishhooks. I think I'll be okay."

**

There was always someone on duty during the night, watching the three exits from the central keep. The Moblys claimed the reason for the guard was to protect those inside, but Justin knew the real reason was to prevent anyone from escaping. It seemed to be a needless precaution, for even if someone managed to get outside, there was little chance for that person to survive the wilderness and find his way back to civilization. Justin smiled. Little chance unless that person was a trained survivalist.

But tonight he had no long-term escape plan on his mind. He merely wished to get outside for a temporary reconnaissance, to find out where the van driver and the guard had taken Mrs. Riggs and to determine for future reference what kind of terrain lay behind and above the camp.

He inched down the hardwood stairs, listening carefully at each step for any creaking or snapping. When he reached the first floor landing, he peaked around the corner to see who was on duty and to determine the best way to proceed. At first, he couldn't see anyone and he thought he might have chosen a night when they had left the place unguarded. But as he examined the room more closely, he saw the van driver

asleep by the fire, a bottle of liquor standing on the

table beside him. Perfect, thought Justin. Maybe the

silly fool had drunk himself into a stupor. If so it would

be easy to sneak out the back door and then sneak back

in later. He crept down from the landing and began to

walk slowly toward the exit. When he stepped past the

driver's overstuffed chair, he realized his care was

unnecessary, for the man was snoring loudly. It was

clear that Justin could have clomped across the floor

wearing hobnailed boots and the guard would not have

moved a muscle.

Justin strode quickly to the rear door and let

himself out with no concern for the noise he was

making. He checked the door to assure himself it

remained unlocked for his return and then stepped out

onto the deck. He was greeted by a blast of cold wind

that made him glad he had dressed in layers and had

worn his heaviest coat. He adjusted his hood and scarf,

felt for the flashlight in his pocket, and set out into the dark night.

He was pleased to see the snow had stopped before the men had begun their drive with Mrs. Riggs. The four-wheel-drive vehicle they had used had left discernable ruts in the dirt road and now it was merely a matter of following those tracks until they led to their ultimate destination higher in the mountains. Justin was now more convinced than ever that the van driver and the guard had not taken Mrs. Riggs to Missoula. He hoped he was wrong about the alternative, but he was determined to discover the truth.

**

Early the next morning Justin knocked lightly on Rachel and Janie's bedroom door. Rachel answered, dressed in a flannel robe, her eyes still puffy from sleep, her blonde hair untidy and falling about her face. When she saw who it was she recovered at once and said, "Hurry, come in, before someone sees you!" She then stepped into the hall and looked both ways to make sure no one was watching.

Janie was still in bed, and when she saw Justin she rose to a sitting position with her back against the headboard and the covers pulled up to her chin. "Did you do it?" she asked. "Did you get out last night? Are you just coming in?"

"No, no," he said, "I've been back for hours. I even got some sleep. I was outside until a little past two." He straddled the straightback chair he had pulled across the room.

Rachel, who had crawled back in bed next to her sister said, "You were brave to go out in the cold."

"I was prepared. Believe me, compared to Alaska, it was nothing….It didn't take me long to figure out what they'd done. I followed their SUV tracks for about three miles up into the Bitterroots. Then I followed their walking trail as they tramped across the snow for another half mile. Mrs. Riggs' tracks were there too, and for most of the way she was fighting them."

Janie's light green eyes widened. "How could you tell that?"

"Because they were dragging her like a sack of potatoes. Then she would walk on her own for a while, and then they would drag her again. She was fighting them for sure."

Rachel's eyes filled with tears. Janie tried to speak, but when she saw her sister crying, she too broke down and began to sob. They both tried to regain control, but they were unsuccessful and their sobs increased. "Mrs. Riggs was so unhappy," Rachel said finally.

"She was a threat to them," said Justin.

The girls regained their composure and Janie said, "Tell us the rest."

"Their trail ended at an abandoned mine. It was boarded up, but I could tell the boards had been taken off and replaced. Some were still lying on the ground.

I made a hole big enough to get in, and I found the

tracks again. They went on inside for about a hundred

yards and then stopped. It was obvious what they'd

done. There was an open downshaft in the mine, at the

end of the main tunnel. I flashed my light into the

shaft, but I couldn't see the bottom, so I tossed in a rock

and it took forever to make a sound. I think Mrs. Riggs

is down there. There were only two sets of tracks

leaving the mine."

Justin watched the twins as they absorbed the

news. They were white-faced and still. They had

shifted their position slightly on their bed and were now

holding each other tightly. He was astonished by how

identical they were. Only their nightclothes and their

eyes made it possible for him to tell them apart. He got

to his feet.

Janie said, "Are you certain she's dead? Maybe

she's alive down there."

"Not possible. It's a hundred feet to the bottom of the shaft, maybe more. There was probably an elevator there in the old days. And I think they killed her before they shoved her in. There were signs of a struggle at the hole and what might be bloodstains on the wall."

Rachel said, "We have to make sure they don't toss us down that hole. We need to put on a good act, make them think they're converting us."

Justin nodded. "While we plan our escape."

"But where will we go?" asked Janie. "And who will listen to us? We're only kids."

"Kids who know where a body is buried," said Justin, "maybe more than one body."

10

New Arrivals

The Prophet J.J. Flack, two additional security guards, two disenchanted wives, a rebellious deacon, and a contingent of assorted brothers and elders arrived at Bitterroot Camp three days later. They all stomped the snow off their boots on the porch, handed their coats and scarves to Elder Mobly and his wives, and entered the great room. Flack's black eyes scanned the lounging area and found Janie and Rachel who were sitting close together on a leather loveseat not far from the roaring fire. He assessed them with obvious satisfaction, ignoring Justin, who sat on a matching chair a few feet away.

The girls recoiled in shock, for there had been no advanced warning of the Prophet's visit. Mobly had surely known, but had not seen fit to inform his charges. Janie slouched lower in her seat and whispered to Rachel, "What's *he* doing here?" Rachel shook her head, and both girls slid even lower and backward into the leather, as if the soft cushions could envelop them and make them invisible.

Justin didn't react at all to the newcomers, except to narrow his eyes and stare at the hatchet-faced leader of the Sheba Temple as if the Prophet were a long-haired demon. Justin then turned to Rachel and Janie, and without speaking, made it clear by his expression he understood what the girls must be feeling.

The main body of the entourage headed for the kitchen area and refreshments, but the Prophet strode purposefully across the room toward the three young people. Janie sighed, Rachel gasped, and Justin narrowed his eyes even further until they were tiny slits in his face. The Prophet stood majestically in front of the loveseat. "And how are my little friends?" he said to the girls, ignoring Justin.

The twins shrugged and sank even lower on the loveseat. They remained silent.

"A bit shy are we?" said the Prophet.

They still didn't respond, and Justin spoke for them. "They're okay, sir. We're all okay. We're trying, sir."

The Prophet turned his head and shot Justin a bored look, as if he couldn't quite place the young boy. "Yes," he said, "I've been told there's been improvement." He turned back to the girls. "I'm pleased. I'll be attending the sessions myself for the next few days….And then, we shall see."

**

That night Justin came to the girls' room and found them both shivering, even though it was quite warm.

"Why has he come?" asked Janie. "Why? Maybe he's come to take us back to Sheba. If he does, we'll never get away."

As was his custom, Justin flopped face down on the end of the bed. "He's brought some new Sheba rebels with him. Maybe his being here has nothing to do with you two."

Rachel shook her head. "He didn't need to come along just to escort them. The security guards could have done that. He came here to check up on Janie and me. He wants us, and he wants to make sure he stays in control. Janie might be right. Maybe he's come to take us back with him."

"We'll be thirteen soon," said Janie.

Justin sat up. "Then we need to get away from here sooner rather than later. We can't just talk about escaping. We need to take action."

With her arms wrapped around herself, Rachel said, "He might let his plans slip in class. We'll have to listen carefully, see if we can figure out what's in his mind."

"I already know what's in there," said Justin. He blew his breath upward, causing his dark bangs to flutter.

"Evil," said Janie.

"Of course," Rachel said, "but we need to know his plans."

Justin nodded. "And we need to get ready to head up into the mountains. I'm already squirreling things away under the slats of my bed, but there's not a whole lot of room there. Let's go over the list I gave you so you can add to our stash. Put the stuff somewhere you can get at quickly. We might need to run on a moment's notice."

**

Elder Mobly introduced the sullen new recalcitrants from the Sheba Temple and then gushed over the presence of the great man himself in the training room. Mobly spent forty-five minutes reminding those present how fortunate they were to have a man of J.J. Flack's stature in such close proximity. Mobly then spent an additional hour reviewing the history of the Flack family and the history of the Sheba Hill Assembly. He began with the split from the sadly misinformed Latter-Day-Saint brothers and sisters, progressed to the Dakota interval, and then pulled his talk together with a thorough review of the present Montana adventure on Sheba Hill.

When the elder had finished his recitation, one of the rebellious wives snorted and expressed her antagonism toward the whole Sheba Hill experience. She concluded her diatribe with another snort and then fixed her eyes on the wall beside her much as Mrs. Riggs had done before her tragic departure.

Justin and the twins reacted with alarm. They exchanged hurried, knowing glances, as if to say that if the newcomer continued to behave in such a manner in front of these dark murderous men, she might very well follow in Mrs. Riggs' footsteps. Rachel intervened. She scooted her chair closer to the wife and said, "Sometimes we need to concentrate on listening. We *think* we know the answers, but sometimes we don't. We listen, we learn." She punctuated her advice by reaching for the older woman's hand.

The woman snorted again and Janie and Justin chimed in with additional input, echoing Rachel's comments and adding counsel of their own. All three young people then got to their feet and gathered around the woman's desk to let her know she was not alone, that they would be her friends.

She seemed to respond faintly, and even

managed a weak nod. Rachel stroked her hair and Janie

held her hand. Justin said, "We're here for you."

The Prophet watched from his chair in the

corner near the door, a pleased smile on his face, a light

in his black eyes. "I'm impressed, Elder Mobly. You

are making progress. Things may very well move

along faster than we planned. He rose to his feet and

moved to the front of the classroom. "Now, with your

permission, I'd like to conduct the next session. Will

everyone please return to their seats?"

His lesson consisted almost entirely of tributes

to his father and grandfather and other assorted Flacks.

He reminded his captive audience of the Flack-God

partnership that had always allowed members of the

Sheba Hill congregation direct access to the mind of the

Almighty.

Though it was terribly difficult, Justin and the

girls managed to feign interest in the Prophet's words,

and were even able to emit several positive-sounding

grunts during appropriate pauses.

The Prophet nodded with approval at their response, and at the conclusion of the session, he announced, "Rachel and Janie Lemon, would you please stay after the others are dismissed? I have something I want to share with you—a surprise." As he spoke, his mouth widened from a smile to a grin, but his eyes showed no warmth or humor at all.

The girls were stunned. They exchanged anxious glances and watched helplessly as everyone else left the room. Justin tried to offer silent comfort as he passed their desks, but he soon disappeared, and they were left alone to face their leering suitor.

"I actually have *two* surprises for you today," he said, standing before them.

"Two?" said Janie.

He nodded. "As you know, God has instructed me to cancel your wedding to Elder Hank Biggars. What you don't know is that God has also informed me you ladies are to become part of my family." He paused to allow them time to express their wonder and satisfaction at his revelation. The thought that they might not be gloriously pleased had apparently not entered his mind.

Janie and Rachel stared into each other's eyes. They, of course, already knew what the Prophet's intentions were regarding their future; but they also knew they weren't supposed to be aware of his plans.

Rachel said, "Your family?" her eyes still locked on her sister's.

His grin widened to show his incisors. "Yes, we'll have a grand wedding, a double portion wedding. God came to me in the night and told me I was to have a double portion in you ladies. And I promised Him I would give you a double portion in return. Each of you will receive *twice* what my other wives have."

The girls sensed they couldn't act too enthusiastic about his announcement. If they did they might come across as insincere, and he would pick up

on it at once. But they also knew they must react

somehow, and without negative overtones.

Rachel took the lead. "We don't know what to

say, sir. This is all too new for us. We're too

inexperienced to—"

He touched her arm and she drew back sharply.

Her reaction caused the Prophet's mouth to default to

its natural cold sneer. "I won't hurt you, dear," he said.

"I was merely going to reassure you that I have enough

experience for the three of us in all of these matters.

All you two must do is trust me, follow me—and by

that I mean submit yourself to God's will."

Rachel recovered and said, "You mentioned two

surprises."

"The second surprise is that when I return to

Sheba Hill in three days, I'm taking you two with me."

11

Preparations

"Three days!" Justin exclaimed, his round blue eyes growing even rounder with excitement and frustration. "Three days. We've got to get busy. We need so many things, and we need to get them without anyone noticing what we're doing."

"We've already got some of the stuff on our list," said Rachel. "In the laundry room, behind the dryer—two packs, one for Janie to carry and one for me."

"I'm building a pack, too," said Justin, "but we've got a lot more to get. And now there's only two days left to finish the job."

"Three days," said Janie.

"No," Justin said emphatically, "we need to give ourselves a safety margin of a day. We need to escape with a day to spare. Let's go over our lists again, and let's start with food—packaged, dry, no canned goods. Cans are too heavy. If we load our packs with cans, we won't be able to carry anything else."

"Noodles, things like that?" asked Janie.

"Right, noodles—all kinds—beans, dried meat. Jerky if we can find some."

"Water?" asked Rachel.

"No, with all the snow out there we won't have to worry about water. We can melt snow. We don't want to eat the snow, that'll lower our body temperature, but we can build fires and make our own water."

"Matches?" said Janie.

"Sure, but cigarette lighters would be better, a

bunch of them. Matches can get wet and useless."

Janet said, "The guards and a couple of Mobly's

wives smoke. I'll bet there are lighters all over the

place."

"And let's not forget heavy clothes," said Justin.

"It's cold out there. Real cold. Three or four layers

plus our heavy coats. Hats or knit caps, scarves, gloves.

Gloves for sure. We've all got gloves, don't we?"

The girls nodded.

"What about a tent?" asked Rachel.

"Great if we can find one, not too big or it

would be too heavy to carry. But I've looked in every

nook and cranny and I haven't seen one. So I guess

that's out. A tarp or two, very light, or maybe a couple

of plastic sheets. We need something to help keep the

cold out of our shelters—from the earth and from the

roof."

It was early evening and they were sitting on the long sofa near the fire. Their words were serious, but their expressions and their laughter were flippant, as if they didn't have a care in the world and as if they weren't planning a desperate escape. On several occasions passersby eyed them suspiciously, but Justin quickly misdirected them with loud silly comments to the girls. "And then the three bears ate Goldilocks and the bears lived happily ever after." The twins' hilarious reactions and Justin's happy face allayed whatever doubts the watchers might have had, and more often than not they smiled at the kids' frivolity. The Prophet was not so easily satisfied. When he strode by the sofa on his way to the kitchen and heard the playfulness and laughter, he gave Justin a stern look and said, "Life is serious business, son. Don't lead these young ladies into foolishness. They have a fantastic future, and they need to concentrate on weighty matters—not nonsense.…I think it might be better if you don't spend so much time with Rachel and Janie."

When the Prophet had departed, Justin said, "I can't believe it. He's jealous of me. He thinks I'm going to steal your affections."

Rachel touched his arm. "You *have* stolen our affections, Justin."

He laughed. "And I feel the same way about you two. But I don't think we define the word the same way he does."

**

The next day's class sessions were particularly trying for the three young people. The Prophet and Elder Mobly harped over and over again regarding the Biblical validity of polygamy and the marriage of young girls to older men.

"The Virgin Mary herself was probably no older than thirteen when she was betrothed to Joseph," said Mobly. "That is our example, our lead, our model."

The angriest rebellious wife said, "That was a different culture, a different time. Who says we're supposed to copy Mary and Joseph?"

"God says," the Prophet interrupted. "He has spoken to me personally and has confirmed everything we teach."

The wife shook her head. "And did He tell you that you can have as many wives as you want?"

With obvious hatred in his eyes, the Prophet stared at the woman for a long time before responding. It was clear to Justin and the girls that the woman was teetering on the brink of destruction and her destroyer was now in the process of formulating his plans.

Justin tried to break the spell. "Didn't a lot of the Bible characters have more than one wife, sir?"

The Prophet turned toward him and smiled. "Yes, yes. We all remember Solomon, the wisest man whoever lived. He had hundreds of wives and many concubines. King David had dozens of wives. And

Jacob had Rachel and her sister Leah." At the mention of sisters, he looked at Janie and Rachel and inclined his head slightly as if to say that his intention to include them in his harem was most definitely based on Biblical principles.

**

The rebellious wife disappeared that night; and the twins and Justin were subdued as they stood on the back deck, gazing up at the dark night sky.

"The tracks head up again," he said. "I'm afraid she's at the bottom of the pit with Mrs. Riggs."

"When?" said Rachel, tears forming in her bottle-green eyes.

Justin shrugged. "Don't know for sure. I didn't see her anywhere after about three o'clock."

"Can't we do something?" said Janie.

"Too late," he said. "And I'm not sure there was anything we could have done even if we caught them in the act. We tried to warn her, to get her to stop criticizing them. But she was determined to have her say."

"We should have told her about Mrs. Riggs," said Rachel.

"She probably wouldn't have believed us," said Justin. "Adults don't pay much attention to kids." He changed the subject. "How are you two doing on the list I gave you?"

"Pretty good," said Janie. "But we need a lot more."

"Not heavy stuff," he said. "Remember we have to carry it up into the mountains."

**

Inside the great room near the side exit, Elder Mobly, J.J. Flack, and two security guards stood talking. Elder Mobly had an anxious expression on his face.

"We can't keep doing this. Two in less than a week. Someone will suspect. Something will get out."

"I don't like it either," said the Prophet, "but God has made it clear He won't tolerate scoffers and rebels. We all must follow His instructions."

The two beefy guards appeared bored, as if matters of conscience were beyond them. They'd been told what to do and they'd done it. Simple. No thought, no worries.

"Mrs. Riggs was threatening," said Mobly. "I understood your orders with her, but—"

"God's orders," said Flack.

"Yes, I know, but today seemed over-the-top, premature. We didn't really give her much of a chance."

"She wasn't going to change, and she challenged me in front of my new brides…in front of everyone."

"What about her family?"

"Long out of touch. She's been buried in the temple for years, and now she's buried in reality." He looked around. "Where are the kids?"

One of the guards, a thickset, brutish man with no neck, said, "Out on the back deck."

"Are they being watched? Can they get away?"

"To where?" said the guard.

The Prophet nodded. He then said slowly, "I don't trust that boy Justin."

Mobly said, "He seems to be making a good deal of progress."

"He's spending too much time with Rachel and Janie. He might turn their heads."

"They're the same age. It's natural for them to be together."

"The girls are mine," Flack said, "and I don't want him around them. Besides, God has informed me that the boy's a troublemaker and that we might have to deal with him."

Mobly's long, thin face turned pale. "Deal with him? How? Surely not the mine. He's too young. We can't—"

Flack bristled. "He's old enough to distract the twins, and he's old enough to go to the authorities if he's not dealt with….God has a plan, and we can't let anyone or anything interfere with His plan."

12

Detection and Disaster

Much later that night, when the household was asleep and the lone guard was once again snoring beside the fireplace, Justin crept down the stairs and eased toward the kitchen. He was fairly certain the guard was drunk and dead to the world, but he couldn't be sure and he was taking no chances. When he reached a position just behind the guard's head, he stood still, listening to the man's grunts and wheezes.

When it became obvious that alcohol had indeed

rendered the man unconscious, Justin relaxed and

headed briskly into the kitchen.

He was on a supply mission. He was carrying a

small canvass backpack he'd found on a shelf in the

upstairs utility closet; and he was hoping to fill the

backpack with dry foods, plastic sheets, matches,

knives, spoons, and even some cigarette lighters and

fishhooks, if he was lucky. The kitchen area had its

own lights, but Justin did not turn them on for fear of

rousing the guard. It was, therefore, difficult to

function in the residual light from the great room. The

shadows caused by the flames in the fireplace danced

on the cabinets and countertops, and on several

occasions he was forced to pause to refocus his eyes.

But despite the dim light, he was pleased with the

progress he was making. In a top drawer he found a

treasure: four cigarette lighters and six matchbooks.

From the cabinets he culled beans, macaroni, and an

assortment of dry soups in handy little packets. On the counter he found a knife rack from which he drew three long blades, including one with a serrated edge which he knew he could use to cut small limbs and twigs. He wished he could find a chopping instrument of some kind, but he supposed that was asking too much.

And now it was time to head back upstairs, hide his stash, and crawl back into bed. He would then get up in the morning and act as if he'd gotten a good night's sleep and as if he were a good little boy. As soon as he could, he would tell the girls what he had accomplished.

Suddenly, the fluorescent lights above his head flickered on, causing him to flinch and to lose his bearings. He dropped his backpack and thought for a moment he might fall to the floor. Instead, he groped for the counter top to steady himself, and when he regained his balance, he whirled to face the doorway. An indistinct shape filled the open space, but Justin couldn't determine who or what he was seeing. He closed his eyes and opened them again, and the shape began to come into focus. It was the massive, bull-like guard who should still be asleep on the sofa by the fire.

"What're you doing in here, boy? What're you up to?"

Justin recovered and said, "Looking for something to eat, sir. I got hungry."

The guard eyed him suspiciously. "Hungry, eh? Then why didn't you turn on the light?"

"You were sleeping, sir. I didn't want to wake you."

The guard noticed the backpack on the floor. "What's that?"

Justin bent and scooped it up. "Nothing, sir, just some books and things."

"Books? How can you read without any light?"

Justin couldn't think of a ready answer, and he remained speechless.

"You'd better give me that bag," said the guard.

Justin clutched the pack to his chest. "It's nothing, sir. Really."

"Give me the bag, kid, or I'll take it from you."

**

Elder Mobly trembled as the Prophet thundered on about betrayal and lies and traitors in the midst of the Sheba Hill faithful. Mobly tried to interrupt on several occasions, but the Prophet ignored him and continued his diatribe. "I told you we couldn't trust that boy. I told you God had warned me about him." The items from Justin's backpack were displayed on the long table in Elder Mobly's office. Justin was sitting disconsolate in a chair flanked by the two burly security guards.

"Maybe the boy can explain," said Mobly.

"More lies," said the Prophet. "Explanations aren't necessary." He motioned toward the table. "Three knives and the rest of these supplies. Was he planning a picnic? The only answer I want from you, young man, is, are the twins involved? Have you corrupted their minds? Have you spoiled my plans for them?"

"Rachel and Janie have nothing to do with this," said Justin.

"So you say."

"What would I do with two girls out there in this weather? I was thinking of leaving and heading back to Alaska. It's what I've always wanted to do, ever since my father and uncle died. It has nothing to do with you, with the temple, or with Rachel and Janie."

The Prophet stared at him long and hard.

**

When Justin didn't appear for breakfast, the twins were immediately concerned. They asked Elder Mobly about it, and his nervous response that Justin was being sent to the Texas facility for more concentrated training caused them to jump to their feet.

"Why? When? What do you mean?"

Mobly coughed. "Well, he has a few issues that can best be handled by our people in Texas. When? As soon as this snowstorm ends and the driver can negotiate the road down the mountain.

**

In their room Rachel said, "We've got to do something. We've only got an hour and a half before class starts, and the snow is already starting to let up. Wherever they've got Justin, they'll be taking him up the mountain soon. There's no Texas, just like there wasn't any Texas for Mrs. Riggs. There's only the mine and that deep hole."

Janie's eyes were filled with tears. She was sitting on the bed next to her sister. "But what can we do? What—"

Rachel said, "I don't know, but we've got to do something, try something. We can't let them murder him."

"They'll kill us, too," said Janie.

"Then so be it," Rachel said, taking her sister in her arms. "What better way to die than trying to save our friend."

Janie wiped her eyes and managed a smile. "Better than marriage to J.J. Flack, I suspect."

"Anything's better than that," said Rachel.

Janie recovered her composure and jumped to her feet. "Then let's get busy. Dress as warm as we can—our heaviest stuff. Extra socks, hats, caps, boots—the whole bit. We can't get our packs from the laundry room. The guard's there, a few feet from the laundry room door."

"I know," said Rachel. "We'll have to go just as we are—except for these." She retrieved a sheathed hunting knife and a small flashlight they had found and had secreted under the shoe rack in their closet.

"That knife won't be much help against the guards," said Janie.

"I know. We'll have to think of something else.
We'll have to get to the mine before they do. Wait for
them."

"Then what?"

Rachel shrugged. "I wish I knew."

"Well, let's hurry!" Janie exclaimed, looking
out the window. "The snow's almost stopped. They'll
be taking him soon."

"Down the back stairs and out the back door,"
said Rachel. "I wish we could get to the laundry room
and get our stuff."

"Me, too, but we have to go now, before they
think to guard the back stairs. We've got to try to save
Justin."

13

The Pit

The girls kept to the trees for the first mile or so

after they left the lodge. They knew they had to stay

off the road that led into the higher Bitterroots. With

the snow abating, their footprints would be readily

visible to the guards who would be driving the SUV

carrying Justin to his doom.

The sky was clearing, but the temperature was

falling; and the girls bent into the still howling wind as

they left the tree cover and emerged on the powdery

snow on the side of the road. They knew they were

now making tracks, but they believed that this far above

the camp, the guards would not be paying close

attention. And besides, the wind was agitating the light

powder, making close examination of footprints

extremely difficult. They continued higher and higher,

always listening carefully for the sound of the SUV that

they knew would soon be close on their heels. They

hoped that before long they would come to the sign

Justin had described, the sign that would tell them to

leave the road and head cross country toward the

entrance to the mine.

Janie cried above the wind, "How far? How far

have we come? How far did Justin say it was?"

"About six miles," said Rachel. "I think we've

come that far. Keep a sharp eye for a small tin sign

nailed to a tree and for the trail through the woods."

"Why isn't there a road, if it's a mine."

"Maybe there was a road and it's gone—covered with new growth. Or maybe a road goes to it from a different direction."

The wind had let up and they were no longer shouting, but suddenly Janie screamed, "Look up ahead, on that tree. A sign, a tin sign. We're there." They raced toward the trail, but before they could reach the cutoff, they heard the sound of a large vehicle chugging up the road behind them.

"Off the road, Janie, quick—into the trees!" When they were safely out of sight, they saw the dark SUV creep slowly past them toward the sign. It then stopped and its lights went out.

"We've got to get to the mine before they do," Rachel cried. "We can run through the trees on the side of the trail. They won't be running, and Justin will be fighting them."

"What do we do when we get there?" asked Janie.

"We go into the mine from the front corner so we don't leave any obvious tracks and then make our way back to the pit. We've got the little flashlight."

"What then?"

"I've got an idea. I don't know if it'll work. But we can try. I'll tell you what I've got in mind when we get there. Let's go!"

They ran desperately through the trees and brush, knowing they must arrive at the mine before Justin and the guards. Whatever slim chance they had of rescuing their friend lay in getting inside first.

As they ran, Janie called out breathlessly, "I hope your plan works."

"It has to."

**

The gaping mouth of the mine was boarded over as Justin had told them, but the job had been done carelessly and there was enough room for Rachel and Janie to squeeze through the corner without disturbing the boards. And because the girls had approached from the side and had climbed over the stones piled high near the entrance, they were fairly certain they hadn't left noticeable footprints.

Once inside, they halted and listened intently for indications that Justin and the two murderous security men were nearing the mine. There was silence outside, so they peeked through the spaces between the boards to see what they could see.

Nothing. No sights. No sounds.

"They're taking their time," said Janie. "We couldn't have been that far ahead of them."

"I'm sure Justin is slowing them down."

"Let's go," said Rachel. "Get out the flashlight. Let's head on back to the pit. I'll explain what I have in mind."

**

Even though his feet were bound about ten inches apart, Justin dug his heels into the soft snow that covered the trail. He also twisted and squirmed and did everything else he could think of to slow his progress toward the mine's entrance. He was determined to make the guards' task as difficult as possible. He had no desire to be a cooperative victim, a willing participant in his own death. He wished he were bigger and stronger so he could put up more of a struggle.

"Fight all you want, kid," said the bull-necked guard on Justin's right. "It won't do you any good. We'll still get you into the mine, and we'll still toss you into the hole."

"Doesn't it bother you that I'm just a boy?" Justin gasped, still battling with all his might.

"Why should it bother us?" said the second guard, an unshaven fat man with yellow teeth. "We do what the Prophet tells us. Flack wants you down the hole…down the hole you'll go."

Justin made an especially vigorous effort to break free and the bull-necked guard cuffed him across the back of the neck. "Cut it out, kid, or we'll deal with you right here and carry you the rest of the way." He chuckled at what he was considering and then added, "But I guess we won't do anything premature. Flack wants you to go down that hole alive. He wants you to suffer—something about God's will for bad boys….But Flack didn't say anything about not causing you some extra pain before we get there. So keep it up, keep fighting us, see what happens."

The yellow-toothed guard said, "Flack thinks you might survive the fall down the hole. That's what he wants—worse for you down there if you're still breathing. He likes the idea of you moaning and groaning down there. I think he's wrong about the hole. I think you'll die when you hit bottom, but we'll see."

"Some fine religion you've got," said Justin.

"God's ways aren't our ways," the guard said, laughing.

"I can believe it," said Justin.

**

Deep inside the mine, near the downshaft, Rachel had finished explaining her plan and now turned to Janie for her reaction.

"Everything will have to work perfectly," said Janie. "One little hitch or hesitation on their part, or ours, and we're dead."

"I know."

**

After kicking the boards away from the entrance, the guards pushed Justin ahead of them into the long horizontal tunnel that led to the downshaft. Justin's bound feet prevented him from maintaining his balance, and after the push he fell to his knees and refused to budge.

"Get up, kid, or else," said the fat guard.

"Or else what?" Justin said. "Or else you'll hurt me? We all know what's in store for me, so do your worst."

The men exchanged glances and then each reached down and grasped Justin under one of his arms. In this manner they scooped him to his feet and began to drag him forward toward his destruction. The flashlight that Yellow Tooth carried was not much larger than the one the twins had used, and the tunnel was, therefore, poorly lit as the trio trudged deeper into the mine. The shadows on the walls danced high and low in rhythm with the moving light.

Justin knew he was about to die an unpleasant death, a death the depraved J.J. Flack would find particularly satisfying when his minions reported back, but there was nothing Justin could do to prevent the inevitable. His life was over, and he now found himself thinking strange, mournful thoughts. He would never go to high school; he would never learn to drive a car; he would never have a girlfriend or a wife; he would never have children or grandchildren. Grandchildren?

He stopped his thought processes abruptly.

Grandchildren? Wasn't that a bit over the top in the

self-pity department? Imagine, feeling sorry for

himself because he wouldn't know his grandchildren.

Ho! Ho! He forced his mind to disregard such

thoughts, and he began to think about his father and his

uncle and even the mother he couldn't remember. Soon

he would see all three of them. The thought calmed

him, soothed him, gave him peace. He closed his eyes

and went limp, essentially giving up his efforts to

irritate and frustrate the guards. It was now time to

concentrate on what lay ahead, not stubbornly cling to

what remained behind. He cleared his mind and began

to prepare for eternity.

A peculiar sound penetrated his thoughts. It

was incongruous, a sound that didn't belong in a dark

mine deep in the Bitterroot Mountains. It was a low,

soft cry—mournful, helpless, needy. It seemed to come

from far away, from somewhere ahead of them, from

below. There was a long silence, and then the sound began again, softer, farther away, mysterious.

"What was that?" the bull-necked guard said, pulling up abruptly. "Was that a human sound?"

"Could be an animal, wounded maybe," said Yellow Tooth.

"Sounded human. Listen."

But the sound had stopped, and when it didn't resume after several minutes, Yellow Tooth shrugged. "Imagination."

"No, it was something."

"Let's get on with it."

But after they moved forward another twenty feet, the moaning began again. They were now within a hundred fifty feet of the pit, and both men halted and stared at each other in confusion. "The hole?" said Bull Neck. "Is it coming from the hole?"

Yellow Tooth flinched. "How could it? There's no one alive down there…is there?"

"I don't know. Listen."

But again there was no sound.

Justin snapped to attention. What was happening? What had they all heard? What were the guards thinking? What were they so worried about? He raised his head and tried to pick up the sounds again, but there was nothing to hear—only silence.

"What's going on?" asked Justin.

"Shut up, kid," said Bull Neck.

They were now moving again, and they were getting closer and closer to the dark, black pit; but they still couldn't see it, for it lay beyond a slight bend in the tunnel. Just before they reached the bend, they once again heard the crying, this time a plaintive plea, a supplication. "That's human," said Bull Neck. "And it's coming from the hole."

"Sounds like it," said Yellow Tooth. "We'll soon find out."

They dragged Justin around the corner, and the

three of them stood facing the foreboding downshaft

that held so many evil secrets. There were now no

more sounds. All was quiet, as if the person in agony

had given up, at least for the time being. The men

released Justin's arms and pushed him aside. Then they

advanced toward the pit, slowly, cautiously, until both

stood on the lip of the hole, staring down into the inky

blackness. "Nothing," said Bull Neck.

"Shine the light over there," Yellow Tooth

instructed. The thin beam made little difference, and he

shook his head. "Well, something or someone is down

there…alive. Those cries didn't come from the air. He

leaned over the edge and called out, "Who's there?"

Still no sound from the pit.

"Give me the flashlight," Yellow Tooth said.

Bull Neck moved closer to his partner. "Just tell

me where to point it. You see something?"

"There by the ledge, thirty, forty feet down. I

might've seen something move. I'm not sure."

"Where?"

Yellow Tooth pointed, and both men leaned forward to get a better view into the pit. At that instant, Rachel and Janie burst from their hiding place behind a long outcropping of rock along the wall to the rear of the guards. Janie raced straight toward Yellow Tooth on the left, and Rachel headed for Bull Neck on the right. Both men were balanced precariously over the edge, trying to figure out what was going on below. With arms outstretched and shoulders thrust forward, the twins rammed their targets simultaneously. The guards didn't have a chance. The line of least resistance for them was forward and down, and they toppled over the edge like two sacks of flour on their way down the storage shoot. They didn't go quietly. They screamed and cursed as if they couldn't believe someone would do such a thing to them. And as their voices began to fade, they called on their God to rescue them. He didn't respond.

"It worked," Rachel shouted. As she spoke, she fell into Janie's arms.

"I thought we were dead," said Janie.

From the spot where he had fallen, Justin called out. "You will be if you don't get over here and untie my hands and feet."

14

Aftermath

"My uncle's favorite word was 'dumbfounded,' and that's the best word I can think of right now," said Justin. "I'm dumbfounded by what you girls have done for me. Where did you come from? You're like two angels sent to save me. What a wonderful, devious scheme. How'd you come up with it?"

"It was Rachel's idea," said Janie.

"Carried out to perfection by my terrific sister," said Rachel.

"I thought you guys were still back at the camp. How'd you get away? How'd you get here first? I've got a million questions."

They were still in the mine, sitting on the cold earth about twenty feet from the edge of the pit. For the next ten minutes Rachel and Janie explained how they had escaped from their room, journeyed up the mountain, run through the woods to stay ahead of Justin and the guards, and then lay in wait to execute their plan to lure the killers to their deaths.

"They deserved what they got," said Justin.

"Maybe so," said Janie, "but I hope I never have to do anything like that again."

Rachel was holding the small flashlight, and she shone it on her own face to emphasize her expression. "I hated it, too. I still feel sick inside, but we had no choice."

"I know one thing," said Justin. "We've got to get out of here. It won't be long till the other murderers come looking."

**

The Prophet's face was sweaty and blotched and filled with hate and anger as he marched back and forth in front of his assembled believers. The failure of the twins to appear in the morning class session had at first irritated him; but as it became clear they were nowhere to be found, his irritation turned to fury. And he was now venting his rage on those who were supposed to watch over his brides-to-be.

Elder Mobly, who had been listening with his head down, now looked up and said, "I thought the girls were responding. I thought we were getting through to them."

"Deception!" screamed the Prophet. "That boy ruined them. Deceit, disloyalty, deception—it's all around me. I wouldn't be surprised if some of you are working against me. Take my word that such traitorous actions will produce harsh punishments, very harsh punishments."

Mobly said, "I don't think anyone in this room would—"

The Prophet cut him off with a wave of his hand. "We shall see, believe me, we shall see. No one can interfere with God's plan for our temple and escape punishment. God has personally come to me and revealed that from my loins will come two great world leaders—two boys, one from one twin and one from the other. These leaders will rule our congregation, then Montana, then the United States, and eventually the world. So now you can see why these girls are so vitally important to me. However, God said only that I would father these boys by a set of twins. He didn't specify the girls' names. So if Rachel and Janie Lemon aren't the chosen ones, it means God has another set of twins in mind. Frankly, I hope this doesn't turn out to be the case. But we shall see. Right now we've got to go out and find them." He turned to his remaining security guards. "Call for help. Get the entire security staff up here. We've used people in Missoula before— get them up here, but only the ones we can trust."

One of the guards said, "The twins're probably on the road, trying to find a ride down the mountain."

"Right," said the Prophet. "Send out all the cars and vans. Find them."

Mobly said, "They might stay off the road so we won't see them. They might walk down through the trees.”

"Okay then," the Prophet said nodding. "Scour the woods between here and the highway. Scour the road and the woods. Don't let them make contact with outsiders. They're on their way down the mountain, that much we know for sure."

The back door had opened a few minutes earlier, and a squat man with a round face, oriental features, a small pointed chin, and the wisp of a scraggly beard stood listening to the Prophet's harangue. His name was Chukchi Zeja. He was a Siberian whom everyone called Chuky, a friendly, happy name that in no way reflected his morose, dark personality. He'd joined the Sheba Hill Temple because he believed everything the Prophet said, and also because no one else in Montana would have anything to do with him. It was rumored he'd spent time in several Siberian prison camps for a wide variety of crimes, including murder, and had escaped to

Alaska, Canada, and then the United States. He was the Prophet's bodyguard and his enforcer. He carried out J.J. Flack's blackest orders and always without question. Everyone in the congregation gave him the widest latitude, and besides Flack himself, Chuky had no friends.

"Not so," he called out. "The twins don't go down mountain. They go up."

Flack motioned for his bodyguard to come join the group. Chuky complied, moving slowly across the room, his eyes darting left and right, as if he might be attacked at any moment.

Mobly spoke first. "Up? How could they go up? The only logical course is for them to go down the mountain—toward the highway."

"They go up," Chuky said.

Mobly and the rest of those assembled all looked doubtful, but the Prophet smiled patiently at the Siberian and said, "Please explain."

Chuky pointed to the back door. "They go down the back stairs and up the logging road, except they go through woods so leave no tracks. I find. I follow."

"How far?" asked Mobly. "Maybe they cut back somewhere in the trees and angled down toward the highway."

"No cut back. Tracks go up, up, a mile through woods and then on logging road. Then up, up. I don't follow. I come back here."

Mobly said, "If they're on the road then Karl and Brian will see them, pick them up—" He stopped abruptly, apparently realizing not everyone in the room was aware of what Karl and Brian were doing high on the logging road.

The Prophet took over. "Yes, well, we'll take a look at all of the possibilities. For now, we need to get our bearings." He then dismissed most of the group and asked Mobly, another senior Elder, two guards, and

Chuky to remain. When the main body had gone, he said, "The boy's punishment doesn't need to be advertised. He deserved everything he got, of course, but let's keep it in this circle for now."

Mobly nodded and stood silent.

"Now, Chuky," said Flack, "Elder Mobly's probably right, don't you think? Karl and Brian should be heading down now. Won't they find Rachel and Janie on the logging road?"

Chuky shrugged. "Maybe so, but why did twins go up in the first place?"

**

The large rock smashed through the window of the SUV and landed in the driver's side front seat. Justin reached through the jagged hole and unlocked the door. "I wish one of us could drive," he said. "We'd take this truck down the mountain, roar past the camp and on down to the highway to Missoula."

"We don't know how to drive, and that's that,"

said Rachel.

"At least we can see what's in here," said Justin. "There's got to be some stuff we can use. It's tough and cold out here, and the higher we go, the tougher and colder it'll get."

"Couldn't we go down?" Rachel asked, "if not on the road, then through the trees, away from the road."

"That's the first thing they'll protect against," said Justin. "They'll expect us to go down. They'll fan out and make it impossible for us. So we go up, not down, over the top and into Idaho."

There wasn't much of value inside the SUV, but they did find a small lightweight silver tarp, a bag of potato chips, and a partially eaten tuna sandwich."

"Yech!" said Janie when she picked up the sandwich."

"You'll be glad we have it, believe me," said Justin. He rubbed his face. "Not much help here. I was hoping for a cigarette lighter. But we'll have to

start our fires the old-fashioned way."

They laid their stash on the hood of the SUV:

Flashlight, sheathed hunting knife, chips, sandwich,

silver tarp. The three young people stared at their

treasures and exchanged smiles. "Lewis and Clark

would think we're crazy," said Justin.

"Maybe we are," said Janie.

15

Into the High Mountains

Justin led the twins about four hundred yards up the logging road, telling them not to worry about making tracks, for he had a minor diversion in mind that he hoped would confuse any pursuers. He then turned north, off the road and into the woods. He continued in that direction for several hundred more yards. Next, he led the girls east, down the mountain and back toward the road until they'd reached a point close to the SUV where tracks were nearly impossible to read because of all of the activity around the vehicle. Then they crossed the road again, this time heading south. "It won't help much," said Justin, "especially if they have an experienced tracker along. But it might slow them down a little."

They continued to track south-southwest for the next four hours, Justin gauging direction from the sun, which had begun to peek through the clouds, and from the shadows cast by strategically placed sticks. He also used his non-digital watch to make more accurate measurements.

"What if we lose the sun again?" asked Rachel.

"Well, I can't be as accurate, but I think I can keep us from heading back the way we came. For example, we look for fallen trees, examine the stumps. Trees up here grow stronger on the equator side—the growth rings are farther apart. The rings are closer together on the side that faces the North Pole."

Janie said, "I'm glad you're with us, Justin. We'd march right back into their clutches if you weren't here."

"What about at night?" asked Rachel.

"We won't be traveling much at night—hopefully," Justin said. "But if we're forced to, and the moon and stars are out, we'll be okay. No moon, no stars, it's going to be tough."

They were hiking steadily upward, deeper and deeper into the wilderness, and even Justin had no idea how many hours or days it would take them to reach the spine of the Bitterroots and cross the Continental Divide. And once in Idaho they still wouldn't know the height of the mountains or the locations of any towns or villages. But the three twelve-year-old adventurers forged ahead, knowing that what lay behind was far worse than what lay ahead.

After several more hours, their stamina began to falter and they stopped to rest beneath an overhanging rock that jutted from a massive granite cliff face.

"It looks like two, maybe two-and-a-half hours till dark," said Justin. "We've got two big problems for now. First, we still need to put as much distance between us and Flack and his gang as we can. They might not be moving yet, but we can't be sure. Second, we need warmth and shelter for tonight. The temperature's already starting to drop. If we stop now, right here, we can use this ledge—pile boughs against the sides and front, build a fire, make a snug little house."

The girls examined the ledge above them and the way it stuck out on the sides. "It looks perfect," said Janie. "Food, water?"

"We melt snow for water, and we've got the tuna sandwich and the chips."

Rachel raised her head to the late afternoon sky. "There's still a lot of light left. I say we keep going, get as far away from them as we can."

"We might not find such a good place later," said Justin. "But I know what you mean. I want to get as far away as possible, too. What do you think, Janie?"

"Whatever you guys think."

"Then let's keep moving," said Justin, "for another hour, hour-and-a-half. If all else fails, we can dig a snow cave and crawl inside."

But a snow cave proved unnecessary, for when the time came to take advantage of the last remaining rays of daylight, a real cave presented itself. It was a neat little hole in the side of a limestone hill. It was eight feet high, five feet wide, and eight feet deep. The latter was important, Justin explained, because bears and other large creatures would likely find it not deep enough for their needs. Best of all, there was a large gap in the rocks above, about a foot inside the entrance.

"We can build our fire inside the cave," said Justin, "and the smoke'll go up through the gap—like a natural chimney."

"What about crawling creatures?" Janie asked.

Justin laughed. "They'll always be with us. We just have to be on the watch for the dangerous ones, like scorpions. That's one of the first things we do wherever we bed down. Check for creepy crawlers and sweep them out of our space. After that, the fire should keep them away."

Both girls grimaced. They shuddered at the thought of scorpions and because of the cold evening air. "J.J. Flack might not be so bad after all," said Janie.

"A scorpion is a scorpion," said Rachel, "and some are human."

Justin was already busy preparing to start a fire. As they hiked, he'd found a small flexible limb for a bow, and now he removed his shoelace to serve as a bow string. He also carried two other pieces of wood: a hickory stick about a foot-and-a-half long, and a flat, dry piece of softwood he'd found under a fallen pine.

He notched a hole in the softwood, wrapped the bow

string around the hickory stick and then strung the bow.

Finally he laid the stick near the hole and looked up at

the girls. "How many pairs of socks are you guys

wearing?"

"Three," they both said at once, "like you said."

"Good, one of you unravel a ball of yarn from

the top of one of your socks." When he was met with

two puzzled expressions, he added, "For tinder, to start

the fire. Then both of you go out and gather kindling—

small, thin, branches. It'll probably be damp, but

maybe you can find some that was protected from the

snow. If we can get the fire going, we can dry out the

rest. Then we need larger pieces of wood, all you can

carry. There seems to be a lot of downed trees and

broken limbs. It shouldn't be a problem. But first the

ball of yarn, and then I'll help you get more wood."

After the girls had gone, he spread the small tarp

on the floor of the cave and went out to search for a

rock or a flat piece of hardwood to serve as a socket to

hold the hickory drill. He found a small round rock

with an indentation in the center and returned to the

cave about the same time as the girls who had their

arms full of kindling.

"Janie's got the dry stuff," said Rachel.

"Good, good," said Justin. He then inserted the

hickory drill into the yarn-filled hole in the soft pine,

capped the drill with the socket for stability, and began

to twill the entire apparatus with the bow string. He

twilled faster and faster, stopping occasionally for a

rest. When he realized no spark was forming, he got to

his feet and said, "It's never easy. Let's go out and get

some logs. I'll try again when we get back. Probably

better to have some logs on hand anyway. Might burn

through the kindling faster than we think."

When they returned, they all carried chunks of

wood of various shapes and sizes, and they dumped

them just inside the mouth of the cave. "Now, let's get this thing started," said Justin. He knelt and readjusted the ball of yarn tinder and then grasped the socket with his left hand and began to twill the drill with the bow. This time puffs of smoke rose quickly from the hole and Justin squealed happily. When the smoke increased, a tiny red ember began to form in the tinder. He quickly reached down and plucked out the smoking tinder and cupped it in his hands. He began to blow on it until it emitted a soft puff and burst into flames. He carefully placed the fire under the driest kindling, and they all watched as the kindling converted the fragile fire into a significant blaze. They waited a few minutes and then added the smallest and thinnest logs to the fire; and after the cave was filled with light and heat, they added the heavier logs.

"That's the bow and drill method," said Justin. "Think you guys could do it?"

Both nodded. "I think so," said Rachel.

"Now five or six more trips for wood," said Justin. "It'll be a long night."

"And then we divide our tuna sandwich and chips three ways," said Rachel, "and melt some snow for drinking water. Has anybody thought about what we're going to use to hold the snow?"

Justin smiled and reached into his coat and removed a bowl-shaped turtle shell about six inches in diameter. "I found this a ways back. The former occupant isn't using it any longer. I'll clean it out, boil it for a good long time, and we've got our pot."

"You're amazing," said Janie.

"No, just trained."

Later, when they were curled up together for warmth, watching the smoke from their fire drift through the crack in the cave's ceiling, Justin said, "This is the best it's going to be. It's going to get worse from now on."

"And we're out of food," said Rachel.

"We can go quite awhile without food," said Justin, "but I've got some ideas."

"Like what?" asked Janie.

"How do you guys feel about grubs, termites, lizards, and snails?"

"They sound delicious," said Rachel.

He chuckled. "And rabbits and snakes?"

"Rabbits, okay," said Janie, making a face, "but I'm not eating snakes."

"You will if you get hungry enough," said Justin.

"I thought snakes hibernated in winter," said Rachel.

"They do, but we might come on a winter den. If so, there might be hundreds of them—rattlesnakes mainly."

"Oh, no," said Janie.

"Not likely, though," said Justin. "But we might see one or two out and about if it warms up."

"How do we stay away from winter dens?"

asked Janie.

"Avoid south-facing hillsides. That's mostly

where they are."

"I hate rattlesnakes. In fact, I hate all snakes,"

said Janie.

"They taste like chicken," said Justin.

16

Pursuit

Chuky shined his powerful flashlight into the pit at the back of the mine. The ancient downshaft seemed bottomless, but he knew it wasn't. He had tossed a rock in and had heard it hit bottom; but it had taken a long time to do so, and he knew the hole was very, very deep. He turned the light toward the rocky ledge about thirty or forty feet down. Was that blood? Had the boy struck the ledge as he was falling? It was a possibility. But where were Karl and Brian? What was going on? What had happened here?"

On the logging road, he had found the SUV with the smashed window. Not too hard to figure that out. The twins had done it, probably to get supplies. But supplies for what? Surely they weren't trying to go up into the high country. They weren't stupid, but maybe they were. And where were Karl and Brian? Had they gone after the girls?

He knelt to examine the tracks at the edge of the

pit. There were so many and they were so smudged it was impossible for him to determine what had gone on here. Surely the boy was gone—over the lip and into the shaft. He couldn't have fought off two adults the size of Karl and Brian. Had the girls followed the trio into the mine? The tracks outside appeared as if they might have done so; but again it was difficult to say for certain because of the snow melt and the tramping that had occurred. And even if the twins had made it inside, what could they have done? They would have been too late; and they would have been too small and too ineffective to have accomplished anything. But where were the guards?

He was puzzled. He knew he needed to get back to the SUV and look for clues on the logging road. Maybe the tracks there would be more readable, and he could then give a report to the Prophet that was meaningful.

**

The main search party had not yet left Bitterroot Camp. The Prophet wanted to wait for the rest of the security staff and for the men from Missoula to arrive so there would be enough hunters to thoroughly scour the upper mountain trails. He was concerned that if the net wasn't spread wide enough, the twins might somehow slip through the mesh. He did, however, send Chuky on ahead with instructions to pick up any signs or tracks and to be prepared to direct the main party. The Prophet also took Elder Mobly's advice and sent people to watch the lower trails and the road that led to the highway in case the girls had doubled back.

Three men from the security staff in Sheba had flown to Missoula during the night and had driven to Bitterroot Camp, arriving before dawn. As directed, they had come prepared for an expedition into the high country; and after stowing their gear, they were now stretched out on the couches in the great room, trying to catch up on lost sleep.

The four Missoula men arrived at nine in the morning. They were not members of the Sheba Temple. Their loyalty was to their own needs and to their own welfare. And one of their needs was money, and lots of it, which the Prophet provided in abundance. All of the men had spent time in the Montana State Prison system in either max or close custody, and all were ready to do whatever their employer required.

The Prophet gathered his searchers on the back deck: the two remaining guards from Bitterroot Camp, the four Missoula men, and the three guards from Sheba Hill—nine men, eleven including himself and Chuky who was still up on the logging road. Mobly and the other senior elders, as well as the women and the peripheral members were busy guarding the lower trails.

"There'll be eleven of us when we meet Chuky," the Prophet said, "thirteen when we find Karl and Brian. That should be enough—more than enough.

The first one to spot the twins gets a two-thousand-dollar bonus.”

One of the newly-arrived temple guards said, “Does that go for all of us?”

“Yes, all of you, so keep a sharp eye.”

**

By mid-morning the three pre-teens had progressed to a position at least four miles beyond the cave where they had spent a cozy, if somewhat cramped night. They had by now worked out all the kinks in their muscles and joints, and the girls were making sounds of hunger and thirst.

“You won’t be thirsty much longer,” said Justin.

“Are we going to build another fire? Melt snow?” Rachel asked.

“Not necessary, listen.” In the distance they could hear a faint rumble, a continuous low growl.

“Is that a bear?” Janie asked in a weak voice.

“No, hopefully the bears are still napping—

though once in a while one will wake up and go for a

stroll. We'll have to watch out for him. And anyway,

when bears roar they stop for air. This sound goes on

and on. What we hear is a river or a stream. Listen."

The growl in the distance was constant, unchanging.

"A small or medium-sized stream, I think."

They hiked for another fifteen minutes and then

broke through the trees onto a smooth, gently sloping

bank that led down to a crystal-clear stream about forty

feet across.

"Can we drink?" said Janie.

"You bet," said Justin. "People in cities pay

good money for water this pure."

They drank their fill, leaning over the bank in an

easily accessed spot near a small pool. When they were

finished, Justin got to his feet and walked to the pool.

"Look," he said, "fish—Rainbow Trout." The girls

joined him and saw ten or twelve fish darting in and out

of the pool formed by a natural rock dam.

"Can we catch one?" asked Rachel.

"Not as easy as it looks," Justin said. "If we had time I could carve a hardwood hook, twist bark into a fishing line, improvise bait of some kind. But all that would take too long. We need to keep moving. I do have an idea though." He went back to the tree line, cut a stout sapling, and began to sharpen the point to form a spear."

"You're going to spear a fish?" asked Rachel.

"I'm going to try."

He stepped to the edge of the pool and made several determined thrusts at the trout. He was unsuccessful, and when the water cleared, it was apparent he had succeeded only in driving the fish from the pool. When the trout returned, he tried again, this time with more and more energy, until, breathing heavily, he collapsed on the bank. "Can't do it," he said. "The tricky little devils are too fast."

"You tried your best," Rachel said. "Janie and I

never did like fish much anyway."

Justin jumped to his feet and hurled the spear into the pool in a final gesture of frustration and defeat. "Okay, trout, you win this time, but I'll get you yet." He looked up and down the stream and shook his head. "Right now we've got another problem. How do we get to the other side? It's running so fast I don't think we could wade across—and we don't want to get soaked. That could be deadly."

"Do we have to cross?" asked Janie.

"Eventually," Justin said, "but for now we can follow the stream."

**

As the search party trudged up the logging road, one of the two guards from Bitterroot Camp asked the Prophet, "How can two twelve-year-old girls survive out here? Bitter cold. Overnight. Food? Water? Shelter? I don't get it. Maybe they're dead."

Flack glared at him.

"Maybe they're in the mine," said the other Bitterroot guard. "They'd be okay in there."

"Then what about Brian and Karl?" said the first guard. "Where are they? Why didn't they bring the twins down?"

The Missoula men and the guards from the Sheba Temple didn't contribute to the conversation, but marched up the road silently, waiting for cues from J.J. Flack.

"We'll see what we'll see," he said. "It doesn't do any good to speculate."

**

Chuky and the search party met at the SUV. The Siberian trotted up to Flack and waited to see if his boss wished to be given the report in private or if Chuky should speak in front of the others. When Flack waved his hand to indicate it was okay to begin, Chuky began to speak in a high, excited voice. "Boy alive. Twins alive. Tracks go up the road. Three sets—twins' and boy's. They go off into the woods, north, tricky,

come back down here, cross road and go south. Very

tricky."

"I don't get it," said the first Bitterroot guard.

"Where're Karl and Brian? Are they after them?"

"No Karl and no Brian," said Chuky. "No

tracks up the road or in the woods."

The Prophet frowned. "The SUV's still here—

they didn't desert."

"Broken window," said Chuky. "Kids do that,

no key. Karl and Brian have key."

"But—" the Prophet began.

"I go back in mine again. Careful, careful," said

Chuky. "Try to figure out, even with bad tracks….Karl

and Brian not leave mine."

Flack blew out his breath and scowled. You

mean—"

Chuky looked around uncomfortably at the large

group of men surrounding him. He hesitated, but Flack

made it clear that the Siberian should continue his report. "Karl and Brian down hole, not boy," said Chuky. "Tracks messy, but no other answer possible."

"But," said Flack, "three kids. How in the world?"

Chuky shrugged. "Don't know." He pointed to the south side of the road. "They go that way."

Flack and Chuky went down the trail and into the mine so Flack could evaluate what his enforcer had said. When they arrived back at the SUV both men seemed certain of Chuky's assessment. "Karl and Brian are gone," said Flack. "Let's get moving…south. Remember the reward: two thousand to whoever spots them first. But we're looking for three kids now. The twins and the boy." He stared into the eyes of the waiting men. "And if the boy doesn't survive, so be it."

17

Survival

As the twins and Justin trekked south along the rushing stream, they could see it wasn't narrowing as they'd hoped. If anything it was widening and producing more and more white water as it sped over rocks and boulders. "Rapids," said Justin. "We'll never get across here."

"Can't we just keep going this way?" asked Janie.

"The Continental Divide and Idaho are to the west. We need to go back the way we came, see if there's a way across back there."

"But we'd be heading toward whoever might be coming after us."

"It won't matter if we're quick about it. We haven't come that far." He held out his palm. "Besides, we've got clouds again and we're getting a dusting of snow. That's good. It'll cover our tracks."

They hurried back the way they'd come; and about a half mile beyond the spot where Justin had tried to spear the trout, they noticed that the stream was indeed narrowing. And better yet, a fallen tree had spanned the rushing water. Justin ran to the natural bridge and said excitedly, "Can you believe this? We can crawl across! And it's high enough so we won't even get our boots wet."

The girls eyed the tree suspiciously. "Unless we slip off," said Rachel. "You've got to remember,

Justin, that we're not trained monkeys like you are."

Justin laughed. "No, no. It's not that hard. Use the muscles in your legs. Watch me. The limb's small enough to wrap your legs around, and it looks strong enough to hold us—if we go one at a time. Watch." He edged out on the log, riding it like he would a pony. After he'd progressed several feet he looked back at the twins and said, "See, it's easy. Just keep scooting until you reach the other side." Then without turning around again, he completed his trip to the opposite bank. He hopped triumphantly off the log and called out, "See! I told you! Now who's first?"

Rachel said, "Go ahead, Janie, you always had more monkey in you than me."

Stepping forward, Janie said, "Well, I'm not afraid."

Rachel snorted. "Afraid? Me? No way!" And she pushed her sister aside and straddled the log. "Here I go." She inched across, much more slowly than Justin had, but soon she, too, was on the other side of the stream.

Janie, having watched precisely how her two companions had made the transit, scooted across in record time, even faster than Justin had managed. When she jumped off, she said to Rachel, "I could've come over and gone back three times while you were crossing." She punched her sister playfully.

"I told you you had more monkey in you than me," said Rachel.

The light snow was continuing, and Justin said, "Perfect. They'll have a tough time following us now."

**

The searchers were hiking south-southwest, but there were now no tracks at all to follow; and they were progressing slowly, not certain they weren't moving away from their prey. Chuky held up his hand. "We stop. We split up. Come together there!" He pointed toward a prominent rock outcropping that appeared to be about five or six miles up the mountain.

The Prophet agreed and ordered the four Missoula men to keep to the present course, the three Sheba guards to head to the left in a southerly direction, while Flack, Chuky and the two Bitterroot guards would climb to the right in a more westerly direction. "If anyone catches sight of them, fire a gun twice. Do we have a gun in each group?"

"We all have guns," said one of the Sheba guards.

"Good. Then get moving."

When the Prophet's group had separated from the others, Flack pulled Chuky aside. "Too many guns. I don't want bullet holes in the boy if we can help it. See if you can get to him first. Break the little troublemaker's neck."

**

Rachel watched Justin as he scanned the heavens, a frown on his face, looking for a break in the clouds so he could see the sun and determine more accurately which way they should go. "No sun, no shadows," she said.

He nodded. "But not hopeless. Remember the growth rings I told you about. I've been checking those whenever we see a stump."

"What about moss?" said Rachel. "Doesn't it grow on the side of the tree facing south?"

"No, actually moss grows on all sides of trees, but you're kind of right. It does grow more on the side facing south, but sometimes it's hard to tell the difference because the stuff looks the same on all sides. Still we'll see if moss can help."

At that moment two white rabbits bounded out of the woods. "Oh!" exclaimed Janie, "Look!"

"They're too fast," said Justin. "We can't run them down."

"Run them down?" said Janie. "Why?"

"To eat, of course."

"I wasn't thinking of eating them. I was just happy to see them."

"Believe me, before long, you'll be thinking of eating them."

The rabbits disappeared, and Justin went over to a maple tree and picked up a small broken limb lying against the trunk. The limb was as little less thick than a baseball bat and about half as long. "Just right," he said. "Throwing stick. Heavy, hard, but not too heavy to toss like a boomerang. But we don't want this one to come back. We want it to bop a rabbit on the head."

Janie made a face.

"I wish I'd had it a minute ago," Justin said, "I could've sailed it at one of those cottontails."

As if to give him an opportunity to prove what he'd been saying, the two rabbits scurried out from behind a white poplar and stood watching the three trespassers. Justin put his fingers to his lips and held up his hand to tell the girls to be as quiet as possible and to stop where they were. He crept toward his quarry, grasping his throwing stick with both hands. The rabbits froze in their tracks, watching him come closer and closer as if they couldn't believe that anyone or anything could be so foolish as to think that rabbits couldn't dart away whenever they chose to do so. At ten feet, Justin ceased all movement and waited to make certain his prey was confident there was no threat. Then he slowly drew back the throwing stick until he was in a position to hurl it with the best possible leverage. He let it fly with all the strength he could muster, watching as it sped through the air toward the unsuspecting cottontails. He missed by five feet. The stick crashed harmlessly into a silver buffaloberry bush and the rabbits left the scene at once.

Janie and Rachel laughed. "You're awful," said Rachel. "I could've done better than that."

Justin laughed, too. "That was pitiful, wasn't it? But we won't be laughing later. We'll wish we had one of those guys roasting over our fire. But come on, not all is lost." He led them to the buffaloberry bush and retrieved his stick." Then he said, "Look, winter berries. They're good and good for you. Eat some and fill your pockets. We don't know what else we might have to eat later."

"We know one thing it won't be," said Rachel.

"What's that?" asked Justin.

"Rabbit."

**

The four Missoula men stood in the cave where the girls and Justin had spent the night. The tallest of the men examined the crack in the ceiling where the smoke had escaped, and then he kicked the remnants of the fire. "Smart kids," he said. "This place's like a Holiday Inn. I wonder what they're eating."

"I don't know," said the fattest man, "but I'm hungry, and this is as good a place as any to unpack some grub." He had thick drooping jowls, and he had a swastika tattooed on his neck.

"Okay, but let's not be too long about it," said

the tall man. Let's find those brats, collect our money,

and get out of these mountains."

**

After moving steadily upward for the next four

hours, the three young people emerged on a high ridge,

separated from an even higher ridge by a massive,

inclined snow field. "Landslide territory," said Justin.

"We need to get up there, to the higher ridge, but we

don't dare go up that snow field. We might trigger a

landslide that would bury us. I don't even like hiking

along this lower ridge, but I suppose if we hurry, it'll be

all right."

They eased carefully along the trail, glancing

uneasily up at the overhanging snow the entire way,

until after a quarter mile they arrived at a point beyond

the potential danger, Janie said, "That was scary.

What'll it take to set it off?"

"Just about anything," said Justin. "Loud noise, falling rocks or branches—or nothing at all. Landslides are unpredictable….So now we go up to that higher ridge. I think there's a broad plain up there, probably a butte. And we'd better start thinking about a place to spend the night."

The butte was not as big as it appeared from below; but from the edge it offered a clear view of the unstable snow field, the lower ridge, and the valley beyond. No pursuer could approach from the northeast without being seen.

"This butte will do fine," said Justin. "We've got to build a shelter for the night. Looks like there's a stand of pine trees back there in the corner, close to what might be a natural rock wall. The trees will hide our fire and scatter the smoke, and the wall might serve as the back of our shelter."

When they arrived at the pine stand and rock wall, Justin said, "A lean-to—we'll build a lean-to with a fire reflector to the side to help keep us warm."

He sent Rachel and Janie off to gather as many pine boughs, saplings, vines, and pine needles as they could find, while he used the serrated portion of the hunting knife to cut long poles. He cut and trimmed ten nine-foot poles and jammed seven of them into the snow and earth, leaning them against the wall. With vines and strips of bark he laced the remaining three poles horizontally across the others, producing a framework. When the girls returned, he wove the boughs they carried into the framework. He spread the pine needles on the floor and covered the needles with the tarp. He used the saplings and vines to patch open spots on the roof, and then said, "Let's all go get more, more of everything—boughs and needles to go under the tarp, boughs and everything else to finish the roof. Then I'll cut some shorter poles to enclose one side. The other side we'll leave open for our fire and fire reflector. And logs, we'll need all the logs we can find, for the reflector and for the fire."

The sun, which had made a late appearance, was disappearing behind the western horizon when they completed their chores. The fire wall, consisting of two rows of long logs stacked about three feet high with dirt and debris piled in the middle, stood just outside the blazing fire; and the reflector performed its function well. The cozy little lean-to was warm, dry, and safe. Nevertheless, the trio huddled together for added warmth and encouragement, Justin sitting between Rachel and Janie. They were taking turns sipping pine-needle tea from the turtle shell. "Pretty good deal for me," Justin said, "sandwiched between two gorgeous blondes."

"I wish you'd hit that rabbit," said Rachel. "These buffaloberries are starting to taste like sour milk."

**

The three groups of searchers had met at their

rendezvous point, and the Missoula men told about finding the cave and about how they had later come upon a swiftly moving stream with no apparent crossing point. They had then turned back so they could meet the others as previously planned.

The Prophet listened intently and said, "My group will take that route in the morning. You men swing to the south and start back to the west about noon." He then instructed the Sheba Hill guards to head north-northwest, also making their turn to the west about noon. "We'll catch the little runaways in a vice."

The eleven men ate a heavy meal that two of the Missoula men cooked on a Coleman stove; and then all eleven searchers gathered around a roaring bonfire. "Break out the booze," said another Missoula man. "It's going to be a long cold night."

The Prophet did not object to the drinking, but he didn't participate.

When it was time to bed down for the night,

each of the men unpacked an insulated sleeping bag and

an air mattress and then claimed a spot in one of the

four multi-room winter tents that had been set up

around the bonfire.

"Like the Red Lion back home," said the fat

Missoula man with the swastika tattooed on his neck.

18

Cornered

"Ground squirrel." Janie rolled her eyes. "If you'd told me yesterday I'd be eating ground squirrel for breakfast and I'd be enjoying it, I'd've said you were crazy."

The morning fire was bouncing heat off the reflecting wall, and Janie and Rachel were sitting inside the lean-to, each gnawing on a piece of charred squirrel.

"More squirrel, please," Janie called to Justin, who was

outside, adding wood to the fire. "More squirrel, please," she repeated.

He stuck his head inside. "That's all there is. I told you you'd like it."

Rachel said, "Tastes like ground squirrel."

Justin had risen before the girls, rekindled the fire, climbed the wall behind their shelter, and had gone for an exploratory trip to see if he could get his bearings. After about a hundred feet he had seen two plump squirrels playing tag on the snow-packed ground beneath the wall. He found a flat, heavy rock, held it over his head and dropped it on the playmates. One scurried away, but the other became breakfast. The girls hated the story, grimacing at the thought of what Justin had done; but after he'd cleaned and roasted the squirrel, their hunger took precedence over their sensitivities, and they ate heartily.

When the twins had eaten and were stretched out again on their mattress of pine boughs, Justin gave them the bad news. "There's no way down, except the

way we came. We'll have to retrace our steps and go

around the butte on a lower level."

The girls pulled more boughs over their bodies

to serve as blankets, and Janie said, "Then we retrace

our steps, but let us rest a little while longer, okay?"

"Okay," said Justin. "In the meantime, I'll go

get us a rabbit."

**

Flack, Chuky, and the two Bitterroot guards

stood evaluating the fallen log spanning the rushing

stream. They had followed the stream south, just as the

pre-teens had, and had seen it widen and the rapids

develop. They then turned around and hiked in the

opposite direction until they arrived at the log bridge.

"The kids must've crossed here," said the Prophet.

"Can we go the same way?" He gestured as he spoke,

his hands trembling with cold and frustration. The

expression on his hatchet face had by now defaulted to

a permanent mask of anger and impatience, and his eyes were filled with dark smoke and bloodlust.

The two Bitterroot guards looked as if they wished they were back at the lodge, dozing by the fireplace.

Chuky said, "Kids small, lighter than us. Log small, might hold us, might not."

The sun was only now beginning to make its appearance above the eastern horizon, for the Prophet had insisted that his group be up and gone before dawn. The runaways might be moving fast, but he would be moving faster.

Chuky had scooted out about three feet on the log bridge. "Seems okay. I go." And without further hesitation he made the transit across the stream. "No problem," he called out. "Come over…but one at a time."

The Bitterroot guards seemed unsure, for they were both considerably larger than the squat Siberian;

but the Prophet ordered them to proceed; and since they

feared him more than they feared the stream, they too

made the crossing.

Flack followed and when they were all gathered

on the other side, he looked up at the sun and said,

"Let's go, I want those kids."

**

Justin felt no sense of urgency about climbing

down the butte, for he was certain they were far ahead

of any possible pursuers. For that reason he wasn't

concerned when the girls wanted to rest a bit longer in

the warmth of the cozy shelter. In fact he welcomed the

chance to grab his throwing stick and police the butte

for signs of snow rabbits. He wasn't ready to admit that

the spooky little critters had gotten the best of him.

And if Rachel and Janie had liked the taste of ground

squirrel, imagine how they'd appreciate a sweet juicy

bunny. When he returned to the shelter an hour and a

half later, he had a smug smile on his face and two

cottontail rabbits stuffed into his coat. The girls were out and about now, and when they saw that his hands were empty, they mocked him and made snide comments about Justin the great hunter. "Going out for rabbit, eh?" said Rachel. "Looks like we'll have squirrel again for dinner—that is, if you can get lucky and trip over another squirrel."

He grinned and reached into his coat, lifting two white, floppy rabbit heads above the zipper. "Roast hare tonight, dears."

They all laughed, and then Justin said, "Let's get busy and break camp. We've wasted enough time. We've still got to get down off this butte."

It wouldn't be long before the three twelve year olds would wish they had left at first light, for danger was fast approaching in the valley beyond the lower ridge.

**

"We need to take a break," said one of the

Bitterroot guards.

The Prophet scowled. "We'll rest when that boy has gone to his reward and when the girls are locked in their room at the lodge."

They hadn't yet reached the lower ridge, but Chuky was already eyeing the massive build up of snow between the high and the low ridge. He had experienced many landslides in his native Siberia, and he had no desire to experience one in Montana. "That snowfield up there," he said uneasily, "I don't like. Maybe we find another way—"

The Prophet cut him off. "You said this is the way they came—so this is the way we go!"

Chuky remained silent, and the two guards exchanged apprehensive glances. "Wait a minute," one said, "if the snowfield—" But he stopped in mid-sentence when he saw the Prophet's cold stare. The possible risk of a landslide was not to be compared with the certain risk of bucking J.J. Flack. The two guards did, however, begin to mutter nonstop, a continuous

inarticulate whine, to let it be known they were

unhappy about where they were being led.

**

Justin and the twins were on the trail that led

down from the butte, well to the side of the snowfield.

"Hold up!" said Rachel, "I hear something. Listen, it

sounds like another river." They halted and listened to

see if they could identify Rachel's sound.

"Oh, no!" said Justin. "I shouldn't have been so

careless. We should've been long gone by now."

"What?" said Janie.

"Voices! Men's voices from down in the

valley, close to the entrance to the lower ridge."

"Who?" asked Rachel.

Justin shrugged. "I don't know, but who else

could it be? They're close on our heels and we're

cornered. If we go down, we'll run right into their

arms. If we go up, we'll be trapped on the butte."

"Maybe we can hide," said Rachel.

Justin shook his head. "They can see us here from any angle."

"Can we hide up on the butte?" said Janie.

"They'd find us eventually, and they'd put a guard on the trail so we couldn't sneak down."

"Then we really are cornered," said Rachel. "Are we caught?"

"Not yet," said Justin, "I've got an idea. First, you two go back up, stay hidden, but near the upper ridge. I'll join you as soon as I can see who's coming up the trail. What I have in mind is pretty drastic, and I want to make sure there aren't any innocent fishermen down there."

The girls hurried away, and Justin scrambled down to the edge of the snowfield and then walked slowly and carefully across the lower ridge with the mountain of accumulated snow looming above him. He could now make out the words from the voices in the valley. "Stop moaning! This is the way we're going and that's all there is to it." He was fairly certain it was the voice of the Prophet, but he wanted to remove all doubt. He reached the far side of the lower ridge and then crept forward until he came to a strategically placed oak tree. He peeked around the tree and discovered he had a clear line of sight on the men who were marching up the trail several hundred yards below. He'd been right. It was J.J. Flack. He could also make out Flack's personal bodyguard, the oily-looking little Siberian; and bringing up the rear were the two camp guards.

He dashed back to the ridge, made another careful crossing, and then climbed back up to the top of the butte at breakneck speed. He found the girls in a small grove of cedar trees not far from the edge, and he told them what he'd seen and heard.

Rachel and Janie lowered their heads. "Is it hopeless?" asked Janie, looking up.

"No way," said Justin, "come on." He led them closer to the rim where three good-sized boulders perched precariously on the edge. "Help me," he said. "Let's see if we can roll these. I'm pretty sure we can get them to move." The twins understood his plan at once. The fear and defeat left their faces, and they pitched in to help him loosen the boulders. They succeeded in dislodging two of the large rocks, but the third was simply too big to budge.

"A landslide!" said Rachel. "We're going to drop a landslide on them."

"If we can," said Justin. His face showed determination and purpose, but his mind was filled with hesitation and reluctance; for he knew he was attempting to create the same catastrophe that had killed his father and his uncle.

**

The four pursuers had now rounded Justin's oak tree and were about to step onto the lower ridge. They looked up uneasily at the tons of snow and debris above their heads, and even the Prophet seemed hesitant to move forward; but his determination returned, and he said, "It's not far to the other side. Just be careful."

"And quiet," said Chuky. "No noise, no talk."

**

The pre-teens waited until the search party was almost halfway across the lower ridge before leaping into action. At that point Justin and the girls began to push the first of the movable boulders over the edge. The huge rock tumbled down the snowpack exactly the way Justin had hoped; and he quickly turned his attention to the second boulder. "Come on, ladies, let's do it!" When both boulders were moving, the trio stood on the rim to watch the results of their efforts. They were devastated by what they saw, for the two giant rocks had stopped rolling about a hundred yards down the incline, and the snowpack had not loosened at all.

"It didn't work," said Justin.

The twins didn't speak.

**

"Look!" screamed one of the Bitterroot guards, "Up there, above us! The kids! I saw them first. I get the bonus." The others raised their eyes to the three tiny figures standing high above the ominous snowpack; but Chuky quickly lowered his gaze and turned to the guard to warn him about the danger of making too much noise. The guard, however, in his excitement at being the first to spot the runaways, had lost touch with reality and with the present circumstances. He removed his revolver from the holster in the small of his back, and before he could be restrained, he fired two shots in the air—the signal to summon the other search parties to the scene.

The mountain began to move, slowly at first, unnoticeably, because the actual slippage was occurring below the surface in the slush and debris beneath the hard-packed ice. But in seconds the entire hillside joined in the slide, hurtling faster and faster toward the valley below.

The men on the ridge knew they were in a terrible position. Should they turn around and race back the way they'd come, or should they try for safety on the far side? Indecision caused them to freeze in their tracks unable to function or to attempt an escape in either direction. When they came to their senses, they all began to run toward Justin's oak tree, with J.J. Flack in the lead. "You bloody fool!" he shouted back at the guard who had fired the pistol, "you've killed us!"

**

The young people watched in wonder as the scene developed below them. "The gunshots did it!" cried Janie. "Why would they fire a gun down there?"

"Because one of them is stupid," said Justin. "I'd guess it was a signal of some sort. They couldn't hope to hit us at this distance."

The landslide had now reached its maximum

velocity, and it was clear the four men would soon be engulfed; but they had not given up and were making a last ditch effort to save their lives. The Prophet was still in the lead, with Chuky close behind and the guards in the rear.

"They'll never make it!" Justin shouted, his voice almost drowned out by the roar of the landslide. "Flack's close, but not close enough. He'll be swept away with the others. Watch." It was a ridiculous command, for there was no way the girls would turn away from what was happening to their pursuers. The disaster below was like a high-energy action movie being screened solely for their benefit. The Prophet lengthened his stride in desperation, and the squat Chuky somehow managed to keep pace. The guards were now lagging badly, almost as if they had caught a vision of their doom and were resigned to it. The wave of snow and rubble caught the two men in mid-stride and lifted them high in the air and hurled them hundreds of feet into the valley.

"And now for the Siberian," said Justin, "and then Flack himself."

But Chuky apparently had other ideas, at least when it came to his boss. A fraction of a second before the wall of snow reached them, Chuky dove forward into the Prophet's back and propelled him out of the path of danger. Chuky himself was not so lucky. He fell face down some distance behind Flack; and the edge of the landslide struck him at the waist, spun him around, and buried his head beneath thirty feet of snow.

19

Blizzard

It had snowed without stopping throughout the day. Large billowy flakes stuck to the ground and accumulated in piles and drifts that made hiking without snowshoes extremely difficult. Each step the runaways took was a challenge—knee deep in slush, strain to extract the leg, and repeat the process over and over again.

"I'm tired and I'm hungry," said Janie. "Let's

stop for a rest and some more rabbit. We've put a lot of miles between us and the search party by now."

Justin pulled his leg from the deep snow. "There's a cedar grove up ahead. We can rest there, but we'd better save the second rabbit for later. We don't know when we'll find something else to eat."

Rachel said, "Rest then. Janie and I are dead on our feet."

At the cedar grove they found a spot where the falling snow was partially blocked by the trees, and they spread out their silver tarp as if they were preparing for a picnic. Janie and Rachel collapsed in exhaustion, and Justin stood looking at the dark sky.

"Boy, would that second rabbit taste good right now," said Rachel. But she laughed to make it clear she knew that Justin was right in saving their food until it might be needed desperately.

"They'll never be able to track us in all this goop," said Janie.

"No," said Justin, "but I'll bet they have snowshoes, and that means they can move a lot faster than we can."

"If they're moving at all," said Janie. "When we saw the Prophet stumbling down the mountain, he looked like he might run all the way back to Sheba Hill."

"Not likely," said Justin. "He'll chase you two till his last breath."

**

The remaining eight members of the search party had set up a base camp north of the valley the landslide had destroyed. The bruised and bandaged Prophet sat under a sloping awning that had been strung to protect him from the falling snow. One of the Sheba Hill guards approached him and began to speak; but the Prophet raised his hand to indicate the guard should wait. "Weather report," said the Prophet, pointing to the radio. "Let's hear what they've got to say."

…And the storms will produce

blizzard conditions for much of

western Montana and eastern Idaho.

If you don't have to go out, remain

in your homes for the next day and a

half, beginning at ten or eleven

p.m.….

"Maybe we'd better head back to the lodge," said the guard.

The Prophet shot him an icy stare, "We're not going anywhere. We've got everything we need right here. We'll wait it out and then be ready to move out when it blows over."

"Sometimes these blizzards are—"

"That's final, no more talk. Tell the others to tie everything down."

"The Missoula men are drunk."

"Let them stay that way. Just so they're sober when the storm passes."

The guard hesitated, looked at the ground and then at the awning. It was obvious he had something on his mind. "Sir, I—"

"Yes, what is it, man? Get on with it."

"Well, some of us were wondering about the bodies out there—Chuky and the others. Shouldn't we try to recover them…maybe before the storm hits full force?"

Flack rose to his feet impatiently, stepping close to the guard until their faces were only inches apart. It was a tactic he used frequently, one he'd learned from his father and grandfather: intimidate your subordinates by smothering them with your physical presence. Don't give them any room to maneuver, and they'll stand like statues until you've had your say!

The Sheba Hill guard blinked and opened his eyes wide, waiting for a decision, but he did manage to insert a short comment. "Sir, the bodies…"

"Will stay right where they are until we're ready to go back for them. Right now they're buried so deep we'd need mining equipment to dig them out. And it's possible we won't get to them until the spring thaw. They're dead, you know. There's no question of rescue."

The guard was trembling under the pressure of the confrontation with his spiritual master. The Prophet had not withdrawn his long, bandaged face; and the guard didn't feel it was advisable to be the first one to back off. Finally, Flack moved away and resumed his seat. "That's all. Tell the others."

"We'll get ready for the storm."

"See that you do."

As the guard was leaving the protection of the awning, he said, "Won't those kids die in a blizzard?"

"Maybe yes, maybe no. We'll have to wait and see. I know one thing—that's no ordinary little boy out there."

**

Justin continued to watch the western sky.

"This fluffy snowfall is going to seem like cotton candy when the real stuff hits. Look at those black clouds building up over the mountains. We're going to get hit, and we'd better do something fast."

"A blizzard?" asked Rachel.

"Probably," said Justin. "I've seen winter clouds like that a hundred times."

"When will it come?" asked Janie.

"Tonight, I think. We've got to get out of the storm's path."

"How? Where can we go? Will there be wind—strong wind? Another lean-to would blow down like the little pig's stick house."

Justin smiled. "You're right, Janie, no lean-to tonight. I've got something much more stable in mind, an old Eskimo trick." He looked around, examining the cedar trees. He eventually found one with a massive pile of snow surrounding the trunk. "This one will do nicely," he said.

"Nicely for what?" asked Rachel.

"For a tree-pit snow shelter. The snowpack around this cedar is fine, maybe five-feet deep. We dig a big round hole, all the way to the ground—even below ground if we can. We use the trunk of the tree for our center pole. We put boughs on the sides and on the floor. The tree above will act as a kind of roof, but we use more boughs and the tarp to cover the hole. We'll be making a type of igloo."

"We can spread pine needles on the floor, too," said Janie. "That'll make it warmer and softer."

"Right."

"How do we dig?" asked Rachel.

"With our hands and with flat rocks and flat sticks. Start looking."

They hollowed a large space around the trunk of

the cedar tree. They dug five feet down to ground level, and then Justin insisted they go down an additional foot, scooping out the dirt with a firm strip of birch bark. Then they packed the snow on the sides and lined the entire space with evergreen boughs of various sizes. The girls then dumped armfuls of pine needles into the hole and Rachel said, "Like a soft mattress." Finally, they anchored the boughs and the tarp on the roof with ten large stones. "Overkill, maybe," said Justin, "but we want our roof to stay put."

"Two roofs," said Janie. "The tree is our roof, too."

"That's the plan."

The snowfall had now diminished, and darkness had not yet fallen; so Justin took the opportunity to build a fire close to the cedar tree shelter. "It'll keep us warm until we have to get down inside, and then we can take some heated rocks with us. You'll be surprised how much they'll help down there. But now we'll make some pine-needle tea."

"No rabbit though?" asked Janie.

Justin reached into his coat to retrieve the second of the two rabbits they'd roasted that morning. "Well, maybe a bite or two each. But we save the rest for the blizzard. We'll be getting awfully hungry down in that hole."

**

At the base camp the searchers were also preparing for the storm, but with considerably more equipment and supplies. With air mattresses, arctic sleeping bags, and insulated tents, none of the eight men was overly concerned about the danger involved; but nevertheless, the Sheba Hill guards went about securing their provisions to make certain nothing blew away or was dislodged by powerful winds. The Missoula men were still half drunk, but the Prophet insisted they peg their tents securely and make certain their supplies were stowed correctly.

The radio weatherman was now predicting the storm would arrive earlier than expected and the advance elements would reach the Bitterroots between eight and nine p.m.

**

The three twelve year olds had retreated to their tree-pit snow shelter. They'd nibbled on their remaining rabbit, sipped hot pine-needle tea, and stayed by their blazing fire as long as possible; but now the wind and the driving sleet and snow had forced them to collect their heated rocks and escape to the protection of their vertical cave. The rocks were effective, and at first the tight little shelter was quite warm; but within an hour the warmth began to dissipate, and the trio began to shiver and huddle together to share body heat. Outside they could hear as the storm screamed through the cedar grove, uprooting any tree that didn't have an extensive root system and then shredding the tree with loud pops and cracks that sounded as if a hunter were firing a high-powered rifle. Justin looked at the thick trunk in the center of their refuge. "I'm glad we chose this one. It'll be here a hundred years from now."

"I'm glad we're in here and not out there," said Janie.

"We'd be dead in an hour," said Justin.

Rachel listened to the whistling wind and moved even closer to her two companions. "If we'd been good little girls," she said, "we'd be in Sheba Hill right now, warm and safe with full bellies."

"About to marry the demon who murdered our sister," said Janie.

At the mention of Mary, their older sister, both girls were silent for a long period; and then Rachel said, "Well, not exactly. If we'd been good little girls we wouldn't have set fire to Hank Biggars' place, and we'd be about to marry a lesser demon."

"Some choice," said Janie.

"It doesn't matter anyway," said Rachel,

"because I think by now we've proven we're not good little girls."

**

The storm howled throughout the night and continued through mid morning; but by noon it had departed and was well on its way, in a weakened condition, to the Great Plains.

Justin left the tree-pit shelter first to start the fire; and by the time he called the girls, he had produced a hot blaze that would warm his two cold, damp friends. After the twins had come out and had spent some time by the fire, he told them he was going out to reconnoiter—to see what damage the storm had done and also to see what he could find in the way of food. He assured them he wouldn't be gone long. He then showed them that while they were still inside the shelter, he'd fashioned snowshoes from evergreen boughs. He tied the boughs around his boots with his laces, and he explained that while the snowshoes looked pretty dumb, he was fairly certain they would do the job. He pointed to two more sets of shaped boughs and explained that he had made snowshoes for the girls as well. He tramped about thirty feet from the fire, turned and called out, "They work! A little awkward but I think they're going to be okay. I'm not sinking in."

The cedar grove looked as if a timber crew had come through with chain saws. Fallen trees lay everywhere. Justin was now more thankful than ever that the cedar he had chosen for their shelter was fat and sturdy, because if it had collapsed during the night, he and the twins would have been ripped out of their sanctuary.

He found a stand of pine trees and managed to knock down some cones with a long stick he found not far away. He knew the tiny pine nuts inside the cones would provide some nourishment, but only from the cones still on the trees. The nuts in pine cones on the ground would be dry and inedible.

He came within thirty feet of two confused mule deer that appeared to be on the same mission he was—to locate food of any kind as soon as possible. He knew he had no chance of bringing down one of the deer, for even if he managed to hit one with his throwing stick, the deer would merely shrug and trot away. But the thought of freshly roasted venison was almost too much for him to tolerate.

About ten minutes later he crossed what he thought might be the tracks of a black bear. He assumed that the blizzard had roused the bear and had sent him out to see what had disturbed his sleep. Justin made it a point to veer off from the tracks. A grumpy black bear was precisely what he didn't need. He also came upon the tracks of a particularly large moose, and he took the same tack that he had with the bear. An angry moose might be even more dangerous than a bear.

No rabbits, no squirrels, no field mice or rats.

All the small creatures had enough sense to stay in their

burrows until they were sure the blizzard could no

longer harm them. He looked for termites and grubs

and insects of all kinds, but found none; so he headed

back to the shelter with only the pine cones he had

stuffed in his pockets.

Back at the tree pit he showed the girls the pine

cones he had knocked out of the trees, and showed

them how to peel away the outer layers to get at the

nuts.

"Not much to chew on," said Janie when she

found a nut.

"No, but eat all you can," said Justin, "and

now's the time for the rest of our rabbit. We'll need

strength for our trek up the mountain."

**

In the searchers' base camp the four Missoula

men were finishing a heavy meal of meat, powdered

eggs, fried potatoes, and energy drinks. The three

Sheba Hill guards and J.J. Flack had eaten a half hour

earlier and were now in the process of putting on their

snowshoes.

The tallest of the Missoula men said irritably,

"This is useless. Those brats are dead—no way they

lasted through that blizzard. They're splashed all over

the bottom of some canyon, waiting for a mountain lion

to drag their bodies off."

"Finish your food and get ready," the Prophet

said. "We're going after them, and we won't have an

argument about it. I've wasted enough time with you

men already."

The tall Missoula man, who seemed to be

speaking for the others said, "Listen, Flack, we don't

see any sense in going up those mountains looking for

dead kids. Give us our money and we'll head on back."

The Prophet, snowshoes and all, planted himself

squarely in front of the bigger, taller man. "Your

money!" he said. "Do you really think I'd pay you for

walking out on me?"

The fat Missoula man, with the swastika

tattooed on his neck, said, "We won't walk out on you,

but we think those kids are buzzard's bait."

20

Capture

Hiking in improvised evergreen snowshoes

proved to be more complicated than the three young

adventurers had anticipated. The fronts of the boughs

tended to curl under, and the backs tended to jerk

upward, causing a rocking motion that led to tripping

and stumbling. Justin tried to solve the problem by

trimming the snowshoes, but it didn't help and the

instability continued. Still, it was better than sinking

deep into the slush with each step.

The sky was a brighter blue than any sky the young people had ever seen, and the snow a whiter white—too white, for they found themselves squinting constantly to prevent snow blindness. But the squinting wasn't working, and Rachel especially was finding it difficult to continue moving forward. "All I can see is white," she said, "even when I close my eyes."

"How about you, Janie?" Justin asked.

"Maybe not as bad as Rachel, but I sure am seeing a lot of white, and I'm starting to get a headache."

"Me, too," Justin said, "but I've got an idea." He led them to a nearby birch tree and peeled off a section of bark that was already sticking out and looked as if it would soon fall to the ground. "Dry, but not too dry," he said. Next, he carved the bark into three masked-sized pieces and poked two holes in the sides of each piece.

The twins watched in fascination. "If those are supposed to cover our faces, our eyes aren't that far apart," said Janie. "We're not hens."

Justin laughed. "You're right—they're masks to cover our faces, but the holes aren't for your eyes. I'm making the eye slits now." And with the point of the hunting knife, he sliced two thin slits into each mask, just wide enough to allow a miniscule amount of light to reach the wearer. Then he went around to the opposite side of the birch tree and peeled off three long strips of green bark, each about a quarter of an inch wide. These he pushed through the holes he'd drilled in the sides of the masks, running the green strips across the fronts.

"I get it!" exclaimed Janie. "Here, Rachel, I'll tie yours around your head."

When all three had secured their masks, Rachel stumbled around on her snowshoes, looking at the sky, the birch tree, her hand, her friends, and everything else around her. "Amazing," she said, "I can see through these little slits, and most of the whiteness is blocked out."

"Snow masks," said Justin triumphantly. "We might look like aliens, but at least we can see."

Janie said, "You don't look like an alien, Justin, you look like the Lone Ranger."

**

At the Prophet's direction, the ex-convicts had separated from the other four men and were headed due west in pursuit of the runaways. They were marching in a column, and they were making good time because of the efficiency of their metal-rimmed snowshoes.

"A fool's errand," said the fat man, who was gasping for air with each step. No way they lived through that storm."

"Fool's errand or not," said the tall man, "we've got to go through the motions."

The man at the rear of the column, who seldom

contributed to discussions or decisions, said, "Why do we have to go through the motions?" He asked the question without insistence, as if he were merely curious and knew his input would not be considered. He was a wiry man in his late thirties, who had spent half his life in the Montana State Prison system. He had no conscience, no scruples, and very little personality.

The tall man halted the column and said, "Because Flack is a powerful man. We don't want to make him an enemy. He knows the brotherhood. He pays them, sends them money in max custody. Remember, that's how he reached us when we first started doing jobs for him—through the brotherhood. The last thing we need is them on our backs."

The fourth member of the group was a stolid, blonde boy from Alabama, who did most of the heavy lifting, and whose primary preoccupation in life was women. All of his lengthy prison time had been as a result of offences against women and young girls; and

he had agreed to come along on the trek because he

liked the idea of chasing twelve-year-old female twins

through the mountains. "Maybe they're still alive," he

said. "Maybe we'll find them."

"Not likely," said the tall leader.

**

Janie sat crying, her back propped up against a

large rock. She was holding her ankle and lamenting

her clumsiness in stepping into a hole and making it

impossible for the trio to continue. Justin slipped the

silver tarp underneath her to help keep her dry, and then

felt her ankle to see if he could determine whether or

not it was broken. "It feels more like a sprain," he said.

"Of course, there's no way we can tell for sure. Can

you walk at all?"

"I'm not sure," she said. "Give me a few

minutes and I'll try. It's really sore."

Rachel knelt beside her sister and said, "It

wasn't your fault. With our snow masks and

snowshoes, it's a wonder we all didn't step in holes."

"I'm the one who did," said Janie, in a fury of

self-condemnation. "I hope I haven't ruined

everything."

Justin held up his hand toward the sun, which

was declining in the western sky. "Each palm width

between the sun and the horizon means about an hour

of daylight left, and there's about three and a half palm

widths now. It's not too early to start planning for

tonight. I don't think we're under any pressure—at

least for today. There's plenty of wood around here

and filler of all kinds. I'm sure we can make a wigwam

if we put our minds to it."

Janie tried to get to her feet to test her ankle, but

the stabbing pain was too great and she fell back on the

tarp. "I can't do it," she said. "It hurts when I put any

weight on it."

"Just stay where you are then," said Justin. "I'll

build us a fire right here close to the rock, and Rachel and I can build a wigwam next to the fire. And tomorrow, if you still can't walk, I'll build a sled and we'll take turns pulling you. We'll be okay."

When the fire was blazing and the wigwam complete, Janie once again tested her ankle. This time she was able to stand, though not to walk, and she called out, "Hey, look at me, I'm getting better! It must be a sprain. Maybe by tomorrow, with a little help, I can hike out of here….But I admit I was looking forward to you guys pulling me on a sled."

Rachel and Justin rushed to Janie's side to express their delight in her improvement. The three pre-teens then threw their arms around each other in a group hug, grinning with the optimism of youth.

No one mentioned the absence of food. To do so would be an unnecessary negative, and they all seemed to sense that what was needed now was positive energy. Rachel took the lead. "How about some pine-needle tea? I'm actually getting to like the stuff."

"Good idea," said Justin, "and pine needles have some nourishment, too—not much, but a little."

When they were sitting by the fire, passing around the turtle shell filled with pine-needle tea, Justin again positioned his hand between the sun and the horizon. "Still a lot of daylight left," he said. "I think I'll go out and set some traps, see if I can catch some breakfast."

"Traps?" said Janie.

"Snares, flat-rock traps—for rabbits, squirrels, rats. I've seen tracks."

At the mention of rats, both girls made faces, but neither spoke; it was no time for niceties.

Rachel jumped to her feet. "I'll go with you. You can show me how to set traps. We can set twice as many with me along….You'll be okay, won't you, Janie?"

"Sure, no problem. The fire's warm, plenty of

wood. I can take care of myself for a while. If my ankle's better tomorrow, I'll help check the traps."

Rachel and Justin assured Janie they wouldn't be long and she could indeed help them in the morning if her ankle improved. They then tramped off on their evergreen snowshoes to find a promising area to trap rabbits and other small creatures.

**

The blonde Alabama boy was the first to smell the smoke. At first he didn't say anything to the other Missoula men because he wasn't certain. It might not be smoke at all, just the natural smells of the forest. He didn't want to look foolish by making a comment that would reveal he didn't know a thing about the wilderness; so he held his peace and savored the thought of two cute young girls sitting by the fire, waiting for him to come to their rescue. After about ten minutes he noticed that the other men were raising their heads and sniffing the air, and he realized that they, too, had picked up the smell. "Smoke," he said tentatively.

"Without a doubt," said the tall man.

**

Rachel was a quick study, and in less than an hour Justin was able to teach her how to set several types of traps and to bait them with seeds he'd recovered from the intestines of the rabbits he'd gutted. Then he and Rachel separated for the next thirty minutes, and when they came back together, she said, "I did fine. I'll bet my traps catch more than yours do."

"That's a bet I wouldn't mind losing," he said. "I just hope one of us catches something."

Finally, the two trappers, satisfied with their late afternoon's work, headed back to the campsite and to Janie. They hiked playfully, lightheartedly, kicking snow on each other with their awkward snowshoes. They teased and laughed as if they hadn't a care in the world and as if they weren't high in the Bitterroot Mountains with no food, no supplies, no equipment, and no real hope.

The first indication they had that something was awry was the sound of soft voices coming from behind the wigwam. Justin immediately halted and put his finger to his lips. "Be very quiet," he whispered. "This isn't right. Janie doesn't have anyone to talk with, and I know she's not talking to the animals." They crept closer until the voices became distinct, and from the cover of the trees they could clearly make out what was going on. Two men were hiding behind the empty wigwam, obviously waiting for Rachel and Justin to return. "They're laying for us," Justin said. He spoke so softly she could scarcely hear him. "Back out. Don't step on any branches."

When they were safely out of earshot, Rachel's bottle-green eyes filled with tears and in a voice quaking with fear and dismay, she asked, "Where's Janie?"

"Gone," said Justin.

21

Decision

The tall man assigned himself and the Alabama boy the task of getting Janie into the hands of J.J. Flack. The Alabama boy said that since the girl was as light as a feather, he would have no problem carrying her down the mountain and that he could perform the task by himself with no relief.

When the two ex-convicts were certain there were no potential landslides to threaten them, the tall man took out his pistol and fired two signal shots into the air; and he then indicated they should head south to see if they could intercept the path of Flack and his party.

For a time, Janie screamed and kicked and pounded on the Alabama boy's back to protest her capture, but it soon became apparent her efforts were useless; and she felt like flea trying to damage a horse. "At least stop carrying me like a sack of potatoes!" she cried. "This is hurting."

He took her off his shoulder and cradled her in his arms. "Of course, little darlin'. I wouldn't hurt you for the world. Sorry if you were uncomfortable." He examined her hair, which was now inches from his face. "Have you noticed your hair and mine are the same color blonde? We could be brother and sister. Do you have any kinfolk in Alabama?"

"Don't be stupid," she said.

"Be nice to me, little sister. I'm the only friend

you've got on this mountain."

**

J.J. Flack stopped abruptly when he heard the two gunshots, raising his arm to halt his companions.

"Two shots," said one of the guards. "The kids are alive."

"Maybe not all of them," said another guard.

Flack pointed toward the northeast. "That way. Let's double our pace."

**

Rachel and Justin were devastated. Rachel was still sobbing intermittently, and Justin was shaking his head in disgust at himself for leaving Janie alone. "I should have known," he said. "Of course, they traveled faster than us on our pitiful snowshoes. They must've tripled our speed. It's all my fault. I'm supposed to know—my father and uncle trained me to know. They'd be ashamed of me for not using my head." He knew he was speaking disjointedly, but he didn't care;

and he continued to ramble for several more minutes.

Finally, Rachel said, "I left her, too, Justin. I was more interested in going out to play than I was in Janie's welfare. I'm a rotten sister. I deserted her, and now she's in their clutches."

They were standing on a bluff overlooking the campsite where the two men had lain in wait. The men were still there, one fat and one thin; but they were no longer hiding behind the wigwam, and they seemed to be making no effort whatever to conceal their presence. "They must think we've deserted Janie," said Justin.

The sun had now disappeared below the horizon, but there was still enough mountain twilight left for Rachel and Justin to see precisely what was occurring below. And there was no danger of their being seen by their pursuers, for they were protected by the branches of a great oak tree. The fat man and the thin man were scurrying around making preparations for the night. They had added wood to Justin's fire and had set up their tent, ignoring the wigwam. "Guess they don't like our shelter," said Justin.

"Picky," said Rachel. "Think we could sneak into the wigwam and spend the night?"

He laughed. "A little chancy, but I do have an idea, a way to slow them down, do them some damage."

"What's your plan?"

And he explained.

**

Janie watched the tall man and the Alabama boy build a fire; and she was irritated at how much easier it was for them, using matches, then it had been for Justin, using his bow and drill. But when the fire was blazing and she was staring through the flames at her captors, she remembered how much warmer and protected she had felt beside Justin's fire than she felt now.

The tall man was now drinking heavily from an

oversized metal flask he had removed from his supply

pack. His eyes were already glazed, and he was

beginning to slur his words. The Alabama boy was

pretending to match his companion drink for drink,

grinning and holding out his cup for refills; but in

reality he was drinking very little and was dumping his

drinks in the snow when the tall man looked away. It

was clear the younger man wished to stay sober, alert,

ready to spring into action when his leader fell into his

customary drunken stupor.

Janie stared at the scene in horror. She knew

what the young ex-convict had in mind, and she had no

intention of allowing him to implement his plan. She

fingered the short, pointed stick she had secreted under

her hip. It wasn't much of a weapon, but she would see

how the creepy southerner functioned with one eye.

The fire was flickering out and needed more

wood, but the tall man was incapable of walking, never

mind fetching wood. His chin had now fallen to his

chest, and the smoke from the dying fire was blowing directly into his face; but he was unaware, oblivious. He sat with his silver flask grasped protectively in both hands.

The Alabama boy was so intent on watching the tall man and on watching Janie, he had lost all interest in the fire.

Though the fire was nearly out, the glow from the burning embers provided enough light for Janie to see that her antagonist had risen to his feet and was moving slowly toward her. He had a grin on his face, and as he approached, she could hear him humming a tune. She wrapped her fingers around the pointed stick that she hoped would at least allow her to wound the thug before he completed his unthinkable mission. With the weapon in hand, she jumped to her feet, wincing at the pain in her ankle, and steeled herself for battle.

He came on with a rush, sweeping the stick

away with a simple backhand and widening his grin as he grabbed her fiercely by the shoulders. She screamed and fought him with her fists; and he laughed, telling her he liked his girls with grit. She closed her eyes in despair and felt an overwhelming desire to die, knowing that such a death wish was contrary to everything she believed, but not caring. Anything was preferable to—

A shot rang out, catching the Alabama boy squarely between the shoulder blades and causing him to fall limp in Janie's arms. She was stunned, unable to focus on what had occurred. She had experienced too much in too short a period of time to organize and categorize the information. She pushed away her attacker's heavy body and fell to her knees, desperately attempting to figure out where she was, who she was, and what was happening.

Into the tableau stepped J.J. Flack, a smoking revolver in his hand, his hatchet face twisted with rage.

He was trailed by the three Sheba Hill guards, one of

whom Flack directed to check on the fallen southerner.

After bending to his task, the guard looked up.

"Dead, sir."

Flack then directed another guard to see to the

tall man who was beginning to stir on the opposite side

of the fire.

"Drunk, sir."

Shaking with hatred and contempt, Flack

ordered, "Take them into the woods, dig deep…bury

them!"

The guard beside the tall, intoxicated leader

said, "This man's still alive, sir."

"Bury them!"

When the guards had disappeared into the

woods, Flack turned to Janie, "How are you, dear?"

"I'm not your dear."

"Not yet, but soon."

Janie grimaced. "At least that vile man you shot

didn't pretend to be following God's orders."

The Prophet glared at her, but remained silent.

Finally, he said, "Where are your sister and that boy?"

"They both died in the blizzard."

"And you survived?"

She nodded.

"I don't think so."

He added wood to the fire, and later when the guards returned, he instructed two of them to take Janie back to the lodge. He explained that he and the remaining guard would head higher into the mountains to rendezvous with the other two Missoula men. The four of them would then capture Rachel and return her to Bitterroot camp to join her sister.

Janie noted that he made no mention of bringing back Justin alive.

**

Rachel and Justin had returned to their bluff overlooking the tent and wigwam. They were pleased with the results of their night's work—which had

turned out to be a combination burglary and search and

destroy mission. They were wearing metal-rimmed

snowshoes, stolen from the fat man and the thin man.

Rachel and Justin were astonished at the ease with

which they'd glided across the top of the snow on their

way back to their observation point. And they carried

backpacks they were certain were laden with food and

equipment. They hadn't yet had an opportunity to look

inside the packs, but they were certain they would be

pleased with whatever they found.

Their crowning achievement, however, was

what they had done to the two mens' boots and to their

tent. And Justin and Rachel giggled with delight as

they watched the fat man and the thin man dancing

around in their stockinged feet, trying to retrieve their

ruined boots from the fire and at the same time trying to

kick snow on the remnants of their smoldering tent.

"Great idea to burn their boots," said Justin.

"The boots were right outside the tent. What else could we do? Putting embers on the tent corners was your idea."

"They'll have a tough time chasing us in their socks with no supplies and no tent," he said. "A successful raid, I'd say….But now we've got a decision to make, and we've got to make it now."

"I know."

He put his hand on her arm. "Shall we keep going—over the mountain and into Idaho—find a settlement or a camp, or even a town? Get help, call the police and the FBI? Come back for Janie with help?"

"Or should we go back now," said Rachel. "Rescue her ourselves, if we can, and then run again?"

"Those are our choices," said Justin.

Rachel didn't hesitate. "I left her alone once, and I'm not doing it again. Let's go back to the lodge. I'm sure that's where they've taken her."

"Just what I had in mind," said Justin.

22

The Run to Missoula

Had the two Sheba Hill guards who had been

assigned the task of returning Janie to the lodge been

inclined to bother her, they still would not have done

so. They had seen (and in fact had participated in) the

punishment meted out to the two Missoula men who

had made the mistake of dealing inappropriately with

the Prophet's bride-to-be. One of the men had been

shot in the back, and the other, whose only offense was

sleeping through the assault, had been buried alive. It was clear that an unpleasant future awaited anyone who messed with Janie or Rachel Lemon.

The guards took turns carrying Janie whose ankle made it impossible for her to hike on her own, and traveling by moonlight the three made it to base camp a little before midnight. They spent the night and were off at first light, heading down the mountain toward the warmth and security of the lodge. They arrived late that evening, and Janie was promptly locked in her room.

Later, the youngest of Elder Mobly's wives, the teenager with little expression in her face, brought a large meal and sat watching while Janie devoured it. The girl's name was Gert, and she was of German extraction. She had come to the temple from Lancaster, Pennsylvania when she was six years old and had grown up on Sheba Hill. She had married Elder Mobly when she was thirteen and had moved to Bitterroot

Camp when it opened shortly thereafter.

"You're really hungry," Gert said.

"I've been living on squirrel, buffaloberries, and rabbit—and not much of those."

Gert hesitated. "You and your sister are so brave," she said.

"Thanks, but don't forget Justin."

"Him, too. I wish I was brave."

Janie watched her carefully for signs she was being phony in an attempt to gain information; but the girl's face was so innocent and so lacking in guile that Janie decided deception was out of the question. "I'll bet you'd be brave if you were put in a similar situation."

"I've been in a similar situation."

"When?"

"I didn't want to marry Elder Mobly, but I didn't have enough courage to run away."

**

With new snowshoes and plenty of food from the stolen backpacks, Rachel and Justin found that going down the mountain was considerably easier than going up. The bright moonlight allowed them to make exceptional progress, and by midnight they were near the area where the landslide had crushed Chuky and two of his friends.

"You think our lean-to is still on the butte?" asked Rachel.

"I doubt it, but we could have a look."

To their surprise, the framework of the lean-to was still standing. The blizzard had destroyed the pine-bough walls, but the poles between the rock and the ground were as sturdy as ever, as if the storm had anchored them. "Terrific," said Justin. "There's plenty of boughs around here. We can re-lace the walls in no time. I'll build a fire and we'll get some sleep."

The lower portion of each of their backpacks was a detachable artic sleeping bag, and as Justin tossed his next to the lean-to, he said, "With these zipped up to our necks, we ought to be warmer than we've been in days."

"I wonder how our bootless friends up the mountain are keeping warm,"

"Who cares?"

**

J.J. Flack and the third Sheba Hill guard also made good use of the moonlight, trekking up the mountain toward the southwest at nearly the same pace they could have managed by daylight. At about the same time Rachel and Justin were crawling into their sleeping bags on the butte, Flack and his climbing partner arrived at the burned-out camp of the remaining two Missoula men.

The fat man and the thin man were warming themselves by a roaring fire, their tent in shreds, the poles of the wigwam feeding the fire. They had no snowshoes, no boots, and no backpacks. Their faces were forlorn, and they greeted the arrivals with expressions of shame and embarrassment. "The kid and the girl, they snuck up on us and stole us blind—ruined us. We can't move—can't go up and can't go down."

"Well, we can go up," said Flack. "And we will—in the morning."

"What about us?" asked the fat man, the swastika on his neck dancing in the firelight.

Flack shrugged.

**

At dawn the next day, Rachel and Justin continued their march down the mountain. By noon they had reached the site of their original cave, and they smiled at one another in remembrance of their first night on the mountain. They'd shared part of a tuna sandwich and some chips with Janie, and they'd all been warm and hopeful, protected by their natural shelter; but now they were heading in the opposite direction, and their prospects had plummeted. At two

they broke through to the logging road at about the

same level where the SUV belonging to the men who

had tried to kill Justin had been parked. It was gone

now and Rachel and Justin assumed it had been taken

back to the lodge or perhaps had been used to ferry

supplies to a point higher on the logging road. They

removed their snowshoes, since the road was hard-

packed snow, dirt and ice. They hid the snowshoes

deep in the underbrush and made mental notes as to

where they'd left them so they would be available for

the return trip.

"Janie'll need some, too," said Rachel.

"One thing at a time," Justin said. "Maybe

we'll come across a pair at the lodge."

They first caught sight of Bitterroot Camp from

a rise about three hundred yards away, and they quickly

stepped off the road so they wouldn't be visible as they

approached. When they were out of the line of sight,

Justin shook his head. "Well, we've come full circle."

"Back where we started," said Rachel. "Seems like a lot of unnecessary hiking."

They both laughed.

They continued to move closer, using the trees on the side of the road for cover. From a point about fifty yards from the back of the main building, they caught sight of the SUV with the smashed window, parked next to a large service truck with a sign that read Missoula Electric. Both vehicles stood in the side parking area, somewhat removed from the lodge.

Justin stared down the hill and said, "I'm beginning to get an idea."

"What?"

"That service truck."

"What about it?"

"Do you suppose the guy driving it is a temple member?"

"How would I know?"

**

Janie and Gert sat on Janie's bed talking. The physical differences between the two girls were remarkable: Gert—dark hair, plump, plain; Janie—blonde, slim, almost classically beautiful. But there were similarities as well: both were essentially schoolgirls with dramatic speech patterns, awkward social graces, and fierce, easily formed alliances and loyalties.

"I've watched you and your sister since you came here," said Gert. "I knew you were faking. I knew my husband wasn't convincing you of anything, even though you tried to pretend that he was."

"You should've told us, Gert. You could've joined our team. Four musketeers are better than three."

"I was afraid."

"That's okay, there's plenty of reason to be afraid around here."

**

After dropping their backpacks in the woods, Justin and Rachel raced across the parking lot and crouched behind the electric service truck. Justin then peeked in the truck's side window. "All kinds of stuff in there," he said, "coils, tools, transformers, big boxes—plenty of stuff to hide behind....Wait a minute." He eased over to the passenger-side door and pulled down on the handle. "Locked, but don't give up yet." He crawled on his hands and knees to the back of the truck and tried the rear door. It opened, and he closed it immediately, as quietly as possible.

"So that's your plan," said Rachel, "hitch a ride to Missoula?"

"If we can find Janie and get her out before this guy leaves....Where do you think she is—any ideas?"

"I'd guess in our room. There's an outside lock on the door."

"Let's see," he said, "the window to your room

is on the back side of the lodge, isn't it?"

"Right."

They took a chance and left the protection of the service truck, running to the side of the building and pressing their backs against the wall. Justin then reached down and picked up a handful of loose gravel mulch from a planter under the eaves. "Come on," he said, leading her around the corner to the rear. He looked up at the second floor. "Which window?"

She looked perplexed. "I'm not sure." She indicated three second-floor windows.

"What's your best guess?"

"You want me to guess?"

He nodded.

She surveyed the three windows. "I think the middle one and the third one. We had two windows, you know."

Justin poured most of the gravel into his left hand, leaving a half dozen pieces in his right. Then he stepped out and prepared to pepper the two windows.

"Time to take a risk."

**

Gert heard the pings first. "Hail?" she said.

"Hail or a bird or squirrel," said Janie. She

walked toward the window, but before she got there,

the pings stopped—and then started again on the

adjacent window. "Odd," she said, moving to the new

location. She was stunned at the sight of Justin and

Rachel standing near the rear steps. "Oh, Gert!" she

cried, and then hesitated, wondering if she might be

placing too much faith in her new friend. But one look

at Gert's open and trusting face convinced her that her

doubt was misplaced. "Oh, Gert," she repeated,

"they're here! They're back!"

Gert joined her and looked down on the two

young people who had been waving energetically at the

sight of Janie, but who now stopped abruptly at Gert's

appearance. Janie sensed the immediate problem and

drew Gert closer to herself with a hug. Justin and

Rachel picked up on the gesture at once, and they both

nodded to indicate their understanding. Janie then

motioned for Rachel and Justin to get out of the open,

to move back against the rear wall where they couldn't

be seen by anyone else who happened to be looking

outside.

"Get dressed," Gert said to Janie, "all your

warm clothes. I guess you'll be heading back up the

mountain."

"But there's a guard right next to the door to the

back steps. How can I get by him?"

"Leave him to me."

While Janie dressed, Gert reassembled the

glasses, dishes, and utensils on the ceramic tray she had

brought to the room. She then described what she had

in mind, and Janie shook her head at the precise timing

that would be required to pull it off.

"Remember," said Gert, "I go out with the tray,

you stand inside the open doorway and wait. When

he's flustered and distracted, you slip out, shut the door

very quietly so no one will know you're gone, and go

down the stairs."

Janie looked into the older girl's eyes, drew her

close, and said, "I won't forget you, Gert."

**

Rachel and Justin were standing as close to the

wall as they could manage. Neither seemed confident

in what they were doing, and Rachel expressed their

doubts. "What now? Janie obviously has Mobly's wife

on her side, but what now?"

"We wait." And at Rachel's impatient glance,

he added, "…because there's nothing else we can do.

We're helpless, and we can't go to her, so she'll have to

find some way to come to us."

**

The ceramic tray shattered on the hardwood

floor at the feet of the guard; and the utensils and

smashed plates and glasses (with a little impetus from

Gert) went flying beyond the guard's chair toward the

end of the corridor. He leapt to his feet and danced

away from the debris. Gert stepped in front of him,

apologizing loudly and repeatedly, occupying his

attention so completely that he didn't notice a small

figure had eased behind his back and was already

halfway down the back stairs.

Gert continued to wail and to belittle herself,

confessing that she was a clumsy oaf, a peasant girl

who belonged on a Lancaster farm—milking the cows

and slopping pigs. But after enough time had gone by

and she was certain Janie had escaped out the back

door, Gert stopped moaning and said to the guard,

"Well, why are you standing around? Help me clean up

this mess. I would never have dropped the tray in the

first place if it weren't for your big feet."

**

Under the eaves, Rachel, Janie, and Justin

embraced, and Rachel said, "How—"

"My friend Gert," said Janie. "Boy, did we have her figured wrong."

At that point Justin outlined his plan, and at his signal they darted across the parking lot toward the electric service truck. Praying no one was watching from inside the lodge, they opened the rear door and climbed inside.

"What if the driver doesn't come back?" asked Janie.

"He's got to. He can't spend the night here," Justin replied.

"What if he sees us?"

"There's a lot of room back here. We'll just have to hunker down. Listen, this isn't a perfect plan, but it's better than nothing—better than giving up."

Less than twenty minutes later, the electrician returned; and after tossing his tools into the back, he climbed behind the wheel and began to head down the hill. Even though the drive to the main highway

seemed to take forever, the stowaways remained silent

and rigid; and it was only after the truck turned north

toward Missoula that their discipline began to wane.

Rachel yawned and stretched her leg to improve her

circulation, but in so doing, her foot struck a steel

container, causing a faint but noticeable metallic sound.

"Hey! What's going on back there?" the driver

called out, swiveling his head to see if he could

determine what was occurring in his truck. When he

didn't see anything, he pulled over to the side of the

road, got out and went around to the rear door.

Yanking it open, he ordered, "Okay, who's in there?

Don't make me drag you out!"

Three small heads appeared at the same time,

and the electrician bellowed, "Three of you! Are you

kids crazy? I'm on my way to Missoula."

Justin climbed down first, followed by Rachel

and then by Janie; and when all were standing beside

the driver on the shoulder of the road, Rachel asked

haltingly, "Are you a member of the Sheba Temple?"

"That bunch of lunatics—you *are* crazy! I fix

their wiring, but if you ask me, it's their heads that

really need to be rewired."

The three twelve year olds exchanged hopeful

glances.

"Do you kids belong back there at Bitterroot

Camp?"

"Sort of," said Rachel.

"Well, all of you get up front with me. It's cold

out here."

After listening for fifteen minutes, the driver

had heard enough to know that he wasn't about to

return the young people to the camp; so he continued on

to Missoula with the kids chattering in his ear,

sometimes individually, sometimes all at once. When

at last they arrived at the outskirts, he said, "You three

are amazing. What a story. What an adventure. I can't

wait till the movie comes out.”

"Don't you believe us?" asked Janie.

He blew out his breath. "It's too wild a tale to be anything but true….Where to now?"

"The FBI," said Justin.

"Too late—they'll be closed, but I promise you the Missoula Police on Ryman Street will call the FBI for you."

23

Trial in Helena

Helena *Independent Record*:

MONTANA ATTORNEY

GENERAL WILL

PERSONALLY PROSECUTE

CULT LEADER

Andrew Bowers (AG) has

announced today that he will

personally present evidence to

First District Court Judge Morrie West in a hearing to determine whether or not John Joseph Flack should be sent to trial for multiple counts of felony accomplice rape for his part in arranging extralegal marriages between adult members of his Sheba Hill Temple and underaged girls. He is also facing multiple charges of sexual misconduct with minors for his own marriages to child-brides. Judge West will…

Helena *Independent Record:*

TEMPLE LEADER BOUND OVER FOR TRIAL

District Court Judge Morrie West today ruled that there was indeed enough evidence to send John Joseph Flack to trial for forcing girls as young as thirteen years old into marriage with his adult male followers. He will also be facing charges of sexual assault on minors for his own multiple marriages to underaged girls. Flack, who is considered the Priest, Prophet, and Revelator of the Sheba Hill Assembly (as well as its CEO) was granted bail in the amount of $500,000, which he promptly posted, stating that…

Helena *Independent Record:*

TEMPLE LEADER

DISAPPEARS—J.J. FLACK

ON THE RUN

John Joseph Flack today

forfeited a half million dollars

in bail by failing to appear in

the First Judicial District Court

of the County of Lewis and

Clark to stand trial for…

Helena *Independent Record:*

CULT LEADER CAPTURED

IN TEXAS

Texas Rangers today arrested

John Joseph Flack on a fugitive

warrant. Flack was a passenger

in an SUV laden with guns and

cash. It is believed Flack was

on his way to his Texas facility

where he intended to set up a fortress-like barricade should law enforcement authorities discover his whereabouts. Also in the vehicle were two members of the Aryan Brotherhood who offered some resistance to arrest, but who were quickly subdued. As to why Flack would associate himself with the brotherhood, it must be remembered that for years he has publicly denigrated the black race as the "devil's vessels." Flack will be returned to Montana where he will be under the jurisdiction of...

Helena *Independent Record:*

TRIAL BEGINS IN SHEBA

HILL CASE

The trial of cult leader John J.

Flack began today in the First

District Court, County of Lewis

and Clark, Helena, Montana—

District Judge Morrie West

presiding. The State has now

expanded the original

indictment to include one

additional count of unlawful

flight to avoid prosecution. If

convicted on all counts, Flack

could face…

Somehow the Prophet managed to look

bewildered as he was led into the courtroom, as if he

had no idea where he was or under what circumstances.

He was a lamb among carnivores, an innocent among

worldlings. He shouldn't be in this place, and anyone

who thought differently was far from God and

spiritually naïve.

"He thinks he's Mother Teresa," whispered

Justin to Rachel, Janie, and Gert who were all sitting

with him on a hard bench at the back of the courtroom.

Also on the bench on the far side of Gert, was Justin's

Aunt Ruby, who had come to her senses and had left

Elder Tate and had stopped the transfer of her Alaskan

property to the Temple. She smiled at the four young

people and was about to lean out and respond to

Justin's comment, when the sheriff's deputy standing

by the double doors put his fingers to his lips to indicate

that the back row should settle down.

While the charges against him were being read,

Flack sat motionless, as if the slightest movement

would cause him severe pain. He kept his black eyes

focused on a spot somewhere above the judge's head,

and maintained a calm, peaceful expression on his long hatchet face. He sustained this demeanor for one day, but on the second day when Rachel Lemon took the stand, he became visibly agitated. His control vanished completely and he jumped to his feet and cried, "A wife can't testify against her husband!"

"I'm not your wife," said Rachel coldly.

He refused to resume his seat, even when one of his attorneys tugged on his jacket. "In our beliefs, a man's betrothed is the same thing as his wife. This woman cannot testify against me!"

"I'm not a woman yet," said Rachel. "I hope to be a woman soon, but right now I'm still a girl."

Both of Flack's attorneys grimaced at the interchange, and both looked hurriedly at the jury to see how the six men and six women had reacted to their client's outburst. Most of the juror's faces were impassive, but a few were nodding their heads at Rachel's declaration.

Over the next three and a half weeks, a procession of prosecution and defense witnesses marched to the stand, including nearly all of the Sheba Hill elders, who testified that their leader's decisions were sacred, since he was God's personal representative on the planet.

"Even when his decisions are contrary to the laws of Montana?" asked the attorney general.

"Even then."

"But wouldn't such an attitude lead to anarchy?"

"We ought to obey God, rather than man."

Seth and Esther Lemon, Janie and Rachel's parents, testified on behalf of the Prophet, even though the twins had told them the full story of Bitterroot Camp. When answering questions about Mary Lemon, Rachel and Janie's older sister, Seth told the court that the Prophet was devastated when Mary died at fourteen after only a year of marriage.

"Don't you think being forced into a marriage with John Flack at the age of thirteen might have contributed to her death?"

"Of course not. She considered it a privilege to help continue the Prophet's bloodlines that go all the way back to King Solomon."

Sheba *Observer:*

PROPHET FLACK

PERSECUTED FOR

RELIGIOUS BELIEFS

The trial in Helena of J.J. Flack, seer, and revelator of the Sheba Hill Temple, is nothing more than a witch-hunt, a violation of the Prophet's First Amendment rights. Though he has tried many times during the course of the trial to explain the tenets of his church to the

courts, he has been continually

ignored and ridiculed, until his

only solace is the sure

knowledge that God hears and

understands.

The support for the Prophet in

the spectators' gallery has been

overwhelming, reinforced by

the presence of almost all of

the senior elders of the Sheba

Hill assembly. These church

officials have vowed to protest

vehemently if the verdict…

**

Missoulian.com:

MURDER CHARGES

AWAIT CULT LEADER

The Missoula Police

Department and the Missoula

County Sheriff's Department,

in cooperation with special

agents from the FBI announced

today they will be filing murder

charges against John Joseph

Flack in conjunction with

multiple corpses found in an

abandoned mine near the sect's

Bitterroot Camp retraining

center. More bodies were

discovered in the mountains

nearby, and those deaths are

currently under investigation.

Already charged in the case is

Stephen R. Mobly, director of

the camp. Mobly was arrested

in Helena and taken to

Missoula to be arraigned. The
task force stated that charges
against Flack himself will not
be made until the conclusion of
his present trial.

Helena *Independent Record:*
FLACK GUILTY
Judge Morrie West has
sentenced convicted felon John
Joseph Flack to five years to
life on each of eleven counts of
felony accomplice rape and
other charges; and Judge West
has ordered that the sentences
run consecutively. The verdict
and the sentencing caused an
uproar in the courtroom by
senior officials of Flack's

church. But the disturbance

was quelled when Lewis and

Clark County sheriff's deputies

circulated through the crowd

serving arrest warrants for

sexual assault against minors

on most of the Sheba Hill

Assembly's older males who

were present in the gallery.

Led off in handcuffs were:

Elder Henry R. Biggars; Elder

Seth T. Lemon; Elder Randall

L. Riggs; and Elder Jonathan

C. Tate. A warrant in the name

of Elder Stephen R. Mobly was

also on hand but not served,

since Mobly is in Missoula

awaiting trial for murder. At

this point John Joseph Flack

was rearrested and charged with murder. Just when he will go to trial on these new charges is unknown at this time. Flack was defiant to the end, screaming that he was being martyred for his religious convictions and that he will be vindicated—if not in this world, then in the next.

"Consecutive sentences?" asked Janie. "What does that mean?"

"One right after another," said Rachel, "and it means he'll be a very old man before he'll be able to ruin another girl like Mary."

"If he gets out at all," said Justin. "He's still got murder charges against him in Missoula."

"I hated to see Father arrested," said Janie.

"Me, too," said Rachel, "but he made his choices and now he's living with them."

24

A New Beginning

Esther Lemon, the twins' mother, had never been mentally healthy, even in the best of times; and the collapse of the Sheba Hill society and the incarceration of her husband aggravated her instability to the point that she had to be placed in an institution for what promised to be an extended period of time.

Justin's Aunt Ruby, who had regained all of her former strength and common sense, invited Rachel and

Janie to live with her and Justin in Alaska; and the twins readily accepted.

It was now winter again, and the three thirteen year olds were standing beside a bronze memorial to Justin's father and to Justin's Uncle Garth. The area that the two men had been surveying when the landslide caught them was now a ski resort, and Justin looked around and shook his head. "Hard to believe it happened right here." His voice cracked and he stumbled slightly as he spoke.

Both girls responded at the same moment, embracing him until it was clear he had regained control of his emotions.

"Sorry," he said.

"No need to be sorry," said Janie. "It's good for us all to be reminded there are men like your father and your uncle in this world. We've seen men at their worst, and now we're standing beside a monument to men at their best."

It was as if Janie had been given words from some outside source, and all three teenagers burst into tears simultaneously. Several passersby stopped to stare, but the three friends ignored them, crying softly without shame.

Rachel broke the spell. "It's cold out here. Justin, do you still have that bow and drill you used to make fire in the Bitterroots?"

He pulled out a book of matches. "I always carry one of these now—just in case."

Janie said, "If the wind kicks up and we get hungry we could snare a squirrel and build a tree-pit shelter."

Justin motioned down the hill. "Better to head for the rec center and get some cheeseburgers, don't you think?"